The Gift of Death

A page-turning cozy mystery of
heroic proportions
Christa Bakker

Counting Blessings

Contents

1

It's too early for this

'Aaah!'

In my mind, that was quite a civilised scream for the horror I'd encountered.

My assistant Thibault, however, practically broke down the door to my bathroom in his haste to rescue me. 'Julie! What's wrong?' he panted, wide-eyed.

From my position against the shower door, I pointed at the monster on the little shelf under the round mirror. 'Big locust. On *my* toothbrush!'

Beau went limp, except for the hand he slapped to his face. 'It's just a little grasshopper. How do you deal with life when I'm not around?'

As the surprise wore off, I adjusted my perception of the size of the terror still clinging to my toothbrush. It diminished just enough for me to take my eyes off it for a fraction of a second to glare at Beau.

'Excuse me? You're sleeping on my side of the courtyard because of some "little bees".' I exaggerated the air quotes as much as I dared move with that Thing so close by.

He straightened and stepped into the bathroom, stretching his hands towards the Green Fiend. 'Yeah, but there are hundreds of them. Or at least, there were, until we smoked them out.' He scooped up the intimidating insect with his bare hands, leaving my skin crawling all over, and carried it out.

I followed at a respectable distance. 'What are you going to do with it?'

'Put it in your bed.'

Raah! I knew it was supposed to be a joke. I knew that. But my immediate reaction was to shiver from top to bottom.

'Can you open the window for me?' He stood beside my bed, his hands forming a ball around the grasshopper from Brobdingnag.

'Here? You're going to let it loose right outside my bedroom? What if it comes flying right back in?'

He closed his eyes with a pained expression. 'Just open the window. It's too early for this.'

Still doubting the wisdom of this action, I shuffled towards the window, opened it, and pushed out the shutters. Thibault stuck his hands out the window and dropped the grasshopper, which plummeted to the ground.

'Oh no,' I exclaimed without a hint of irony. 'I hope he hasn't hurt himself.'

Beau only sighed as he fixed the shutters to the wall outside. 'Will you be all right, or should I call someone from the trauma team?'

When I didn't dignify his question with a response, he added, 'You woke me up from a great dream.'

'Did it involve Céline?'

His surprised gape negated the pleasing effect of the morning breeze playing with his blond mop.

I rolled my eyes. 'Oh please, you don't need to be Sherlock Holmes for that one. Besides, you told me.'

Rubbing his eyes, he pushed past me on his way out of the room. 'I know. But I was hoping you'd have forgotten about that.'

'*Aucune chance.*' It was probably just as well he didn't see the enormous grin I sent to the back of his head. We hadn't talked about – or even mentioned – his crush on the baker's daughter since he confessed it at Easter. It was now July. This was a tremendous sacrifice on my part, but as I had been about to throw him out of my house after his snarky remark about the trauma team, mentioning her was the best compromise I could make.

'Since I'm awake,' he called from halfway down the stairs, 'I might as well go to the *boulangerie*. You want anything for later?'

I suppressed the urge to sing about the baker's daughter being at the bakery and very maturely answered, 'No, I'll be at the hotel later, so I can do it myself.'

He uttered something that sounded like *d'accord*, but since he was already downstairs by then, I assumed it more than I heard it. Suspiciously eyeing the shelf under the mirror, I entered the bathroom once more. That toothbrush would grace the landfill soon. But as I bought bamboo ones, I wasn't too sorry for the Earth. Were grasshoppers particularly attracted to bamboo? In that case, I might have to rethink my reduction of the use of plastics.

Making a mental note to look this up, I took a new toothbrush from its wrapper and thought about my day. My client yesterday had been eighty-three years old. As sprightly as she was, she did have the wrinkles to go with her age, and not just on her face, if you get my drift. She'd been perfectly willing to show her frilly granny pants, but I now had a good amount of editing to do. Not that I was going to polish her up completely, but she had to look in the picture the way she'd felt during the day, which was just a few years younger than reality showed.

But before I started work, I'd have to pay a visit to the hotel in the village. Though I was supposed to be a silent partner, my friend Jeanette Ta often asked me for my advice and help in certain matters. The hotel had only been open for a couple of months, but already we were dealing with a major event. One of the most important global film celebrations, the Gala des Lumières, had just taken place in Lyon, and four of its famous attendees had decided to extend their stay. In our hotel. And of course they happened to be my best friend Tiana's absolute heroes.

Literally. These four played superheroes in one of the most successful film series in its genre. Tiana had asked me to join her at various events surrounding the Gala, which I'd managed to dodge, but now I had to go and meet them after all. And I knew nothing about them. Perhaps I should stop in at Tiana's on my way to pick up some pointers on how to deal with these men.

Determined to at least look professional, I selected my black cropped trousers and matching simple blouse with a pair of shiny Oxfords. With my hair in a low ponytail, I couldn't have looked more French if I'd worn a beret. By the time I'd done my make-up, Beau was home with breakfast, and I went down to make coffee.

'One more month,' I declared.

'To the day,' Beau finished for me.

I grinned at him. 'Do I say it too often?'

'Every single day. Multiple times. Just in case I didn't get it from the calendar.' With an indulgent smile, he pointed at the kitchen wall, where a calendar had been open to August for months now, the tenth circled in thick red ink with the words LÉON RETURNS written on top, followed by several exclamation marks for good measure. If possible, I had only grown more smitten with the dusty economics professor, even though we only talked late at night because he was teaching in Michigan. For now.

Since Beau seemed in a good mood, I dared ask a seemingly innocent question. 'So how is Céline today?'

He'd just been to the bakery. It could have been a polite remark and nothing more. Which is what I was prepared to defend in case he accused me of prying. Instead, he looked me in the eye over his coffee mug, took a long sip, then sighed and dropped all pretence. 'Amazing, as always.'

I jumped on it with all the curiosity that had been building since Easter, though I needed to be careful not to scare him off. 'I don't get it. Her boyfriend gets jealous because she embraces you in the middle of the café – which wasn't all that strange since you'd just been shot – so she breaks up with him. And still you do nothing about it. They broke up. Because of you! And yet, here you are sighing.'

Okay, so maybe I was just super curious and not all that careful. But it had to be said.

He stared at the coffee mug in his hands. 'She just wants to be friends. She said so, years ago. And again after she broke up with him, claiming he was being jealous for no good reason because there was nothing more than friendship between us.' He twisted his voice, but his imitation of Céline lacked some of the mocking accuracy of his other impressions. 'He was jealous, which is ridiculous. You and I are just friends. He should know that.' He sighed again. '*Eh ben*, I'm always there. If her feelings ever change, I'll notice, *non*?'

I had nothing to say to that. Even if I could think of something, I didn't want to poke a wound that was clearly painful. I glanced at the calendar. While I was looking forward to Léon's return, he and I had quite the past too. 'What a pair we are.'

He huffed, but it wasn't really a laugh. We drank our coffee in silence, but though I felt for him and would love to spend the hours dreaming about Léon, my thoughts drifted towards the day ahead. I'd scheduled a couple of days without shoots so I could give my full attention to Jeanette, should she need it. As a matter of fact, though, I hoped she didn't. I could use a few days just lying in the sun. Well, mornings, of course, now that it was summer. Only 'mad dogs and Englishmen' as they say...

Apparently, one or two of the film stars were British. I really should find out more about them. I checked my watch. Would Tiana be awake already? As a writer, she could fill in her own hours, which in her case meant late mornings. I decided to throw caution to the wind and simply drop in on her. Making Beau dodge by reaching out in a pretend attempt to ruffle his hair, I got up and put my phone in my purse. 'Any plans for the day?' I asked my own superhero.

Beau shrugged, which was all I would get.

'All right, have fun with that. *Tomates farcies* for lunch, if you're here.'

Patting the lion's head doorknob as I closed the door behind me, I set off on the path towards Tiana's house. As I made my way up the steep path, I breathed in deep. The dry scent of the trees around me mingled with that of cut grass rolling down the slope from a garden further up the hill. The church bell chimed nine. Surely nine wouldn't be too early for Tiana?

The steep woodland path led onto the little road that ended at the two houses belonging to Tiana and her neighbours, Catherine and Daniel. Both houses were new, but traditionally built with the region's golden yellow stone. A low wall on the opposite side of the street separated the houses from a vineyard that once belonged to my family but had long since been sold on.

'Why are you here? You should be with them.' Tiana panted slightly as she opened the door. Ordinarily, the door was unlocked and I simply entered, so she must have seen me coming through the kitchen window. 'Are they here? Have you seen Will yet?'

'Ti...' She'd been a terrible friend lately. When she found out those film stars were coming to France, she absolutely had to have tickets to every single event they would be at. She dragged her boyfriend to the red carpet, where she camped out early in the morning, just to have a good spot in the evening. Lucas was into all of that comic-y stuff too, but even he was getting fed up. I'd caught him rolling his eyes several times already when she started on how handsome Will Rice was, and how he must be a good person or he couldn't play one so convincingly.

Tiana buzzed with excitement whenever she spoke about these superhero movies, but Wilbraham Rice, who played Captain Canon, was her particular favourite.

'Is he really that tall and muscular?' she asked now.

I had to suppress an eye-roll myself. *All* these men were tall, good-looking, and muscular. They played superheroes.

'Hello to you, too. Nice to see you so calm today.' I had to physically push her out of the way to get indoors. 'They won't be here until ten, at least. And then they'll have to settle in before I can get them dressed up in frilly skirts.'

Tiana stared, her mouth slightly open.

'That's not a good look on you. Also, you usually laugh at my jokes.'

'Oh. Oh! Ah! I see, funny.'

'Have you slept at all?' The last events surrounding the Gala des Lumières had finished two days ago, which would have returned Tiana to normal, had it not been for Jeanette. I'd expressly told her not to mention the fact that the actors would be staying at our hotel, but she was only slightly less excited than Tiana. When Tiana and I were having lunch at the hotel the day before, we'd been within earshot of Jeanette – which frankly meant anywhere in the restaurant at that volume – when she instructed her staff on how to behave when the Hollywood stars would be there. Tiana had almost died.

'Who needs sleep? I have to be ready by ten, so I can just-happen-to-be there.'

Taking Tiana by both arms, I guided her towards the sofa. 'Ti, you're scaring me. Sit down and have some *tisane* or something. Here, a comic. That'll keep you busy while I put the kettle on.'

I shoved some colourful magazine into her hands and shook my head all the way to the kitchen. These guys had better leave soon, or my friend would not survive. While waiting for the water to boil, I stared out the kitchen window. The neighbours' old Labrador was sniffing around the low wall. Suddenly, it whimpered and plastered itself to the stones.

I frowned, leaning forward to see what could have caused such fear in the poor dog. At first, nothing stood out, but then a man with a huge belly appeared. He was so big, he used a small electrical extension cord for his belt. I'd seen him around the village but didn't know him. If old Banzaï was so afraid of him, however, that didn't bode well for his character.

The man passed and the kettle clicked off. 'So we're clear? You're not going to sneak up on my guests?' I asked as I returned to the living room. Tiana softly snored in answer.

2

You've got a nerve!

Having covered Tiana with a light blanket, I trudged down the road towards the village. Though my destination was eventually the hotel, my first stop was the butcher's. I thought I'd beat the crowd if I went in early, but I was wrong. The bell tinkled overhead as I pushed open the door to the little shop and was assaulted with questions by half the village, none of them there for their lunch meats. The butcher's had always been the centre of any kind of gossip, and by now everyone was aware of my famous guests.

'How long have you known?' was Isabelle Cochon's greeting to me as she handed a customer her meat.

'Good to see you back,' I replied. 'How have you been?'

Isabelle had been away for several weeks, and nobody seemed to know where she'd gone. In her absence, the village's biggest gossip had become its hottest topic of speculation and suggestion. But with the Hollywood stars staying at my hotel, she'd chosen the right moment to return and not be the target of everyone's talk. No one seemed to have even heard my jab.

'Are they staying for long?'

'Can I get an autograph?'

'I liked him in *The Duke Who Claimed Me*.'

'Who, Monty? Wasn't that the bigamy film?'

'I heard he had someone on the side in real life as well.'

'No, wasn't that Ben Hjerson? His wife's been looking miserable in photos lately.'

Isabelle huffed, planting a fist on her curvy hip. 'If you can get arrested for bigamy, shouldn't cheating come with at least a nice big fine? Paid to the spouse. Or community service. Also to the spouse.'

Several people murmured agreement. Sophia Labouche, a childhood friend of mine whom I'd lost contact with apart from the occasional greeting, ran a hand through her shiny, brown hair. 'Or you could simply find someone who doesn't cheat.'

One day, I'd expand on the passing greeting and see if we still had anything in common now that she was part of the Perfect School Mums team, but today was not that day.

Isabelle lifted an eyebrow but mostly ignored her. Madame Dufaux, another village regular, stroked her frizzy mane. 'Hm. Mine uses the bread board to cut the vegetables, but at least that means no one else would want him.'

The bell above the door tinkled again, and Isabelle's face contorted with rage. '*Toi!* You've got a nerve!'

Everyone, including me, turned towards the new arrival. It was the man with the monumental circumference I'd seen passing Tiana's house.

Isabelle turned and grabbed a stale baguette she normally used for breadcrumbs. Wielding the thing high above her head with one powerful arm, she stormed around the counter with a battle cry worthy of Boudicca. Epic Belly Man stood nailed to the spot as she plunged her baguette sword into his stomach, to collective gasps from the audience. He turned pink, then red, then purple, garbled some outraged words but then fell silent and paled, his eyes bulging and his broad fingers clutching the spot where Isabelle had poked him. Without another word, he turned and left the shop.

'Do you think he's all right?' Sophia asked.

'What do you think?' Isabelle scoffed. 'He'll have to get his meat from the supermarket from now on.'

A terrible fate indeed. I wondered, as did probably everyone else in the shop, what Epic Belly Man could have done to deserve this much fury, but nobody dared ask.

'I'd like some mince, please,' I offered instead.

With that, most of the shoppers dispersed, muttering *'Oh, la vache!'*, *'Bon sang!'* and long strings of *'Oh, là là là!'*, and setting off to other venues to gossip about this latest bit of excitement without its subject present.

'Will that be all?'

Mais non, of course not. Tell me all the juicy news! But then, I was not a gossip. That kind of shortcoming was reserved for those less fortunate. 'Yes, thanks. I do hope you won't get into trouble because of... him.'

'Pfff! Monsieur Louis Lutz doesn't scare me. If anything, he should be scared of me.'

Another intriguing declaration. I thanked her and left the shop, drinking in the summer air filled with the scent of flowers and yellow dust from the gravelly square. This side of our magnificent church was in shadows, as usual around this time of day, but the sun's rays sparked fire in the water droplets of the fountain in the middle of the square. Beyond it, on a bench overlooking the steep slope down towards the *pétanque* court, sat Louis Lutz, his expansive midriff rising and falling rapidly and with apparently considerable difficulty. His wheezing breath made me stop to see if he needed help, but as soon as I rounded the bench and looked his way, I remembered why I didn't like him. Every time he looked at me, it was as if he looked through me. If that had meant he saw through me, or he looked into my soul, that would have been disconcerting enough, but he looked through me as if I didn't exist.

'Are you all right?' I asked despite my reservations.

No response. None at all. Not even a blink.

'Do you need help?' I tried again.

This time he narrowed his eyes and actually looked at me. 'From whom? You? I don't think so. Go away, Butt Lady.'

I hadn't heard that nickname in months, though I knew it was what the children at the village school called me. Part of me wanted to rebel, stay when he told me to go, but why would I help someone who clearly did not want me around? I could use my time better, so I turned towards the hotel and walked away without a second glance. It was half past nine. Time to face the music.

Looking up at the front of the hotel that was Jeanette's pet project but had brought me mostly headaches, I brushed imaginary dust off my blouse before I entered the revolving doors. Now was not the time to worry about empty rooms or broken crockery. I finally got to enjoy the company of the guests instead. While that had in fact been one of the main reasons for me to be a silent partner – that I wouldn't have to deal with the whims of holiday-goers – it now seemed a welcome change from only dealing with the administrative side of things.

As always when I entered the building, I marvelled at the change Jeanette had brought about. Gone were the dark wooden slats and the dirty orange carpet. In its place were soft pink marble tiles and lots of greenery everywhere. It even smelled fresh and floral. Next to the entrance was a little table with sparklingly clean glasses and a pitcher of water that the villagers had already discovered and made ready use of now the warmer months had arrived. The closing of the café had caused quite a stir at first, but when people found out the hotel's restaurant would serve them the same good food for the same prices in a much improved environment, the murmur had quickly died down.

Now, the hotel lounge was filled to bursting. I hadn't seen it this full since before we renovated and were about to remove an ugly mural the previous owners had commissioned. Though that turned out to be lucrative in the end, this crowd would probably not make us much money. They were here for one thing only. Well... four 'things'. But they weren't due for another half hour.

So when I approached a shakingly nervous Jeanette at the reception desk and the chatter behind me grew to an excited buzz, I did not expect it to be about the movie stars. However, when Jeanette looked over my shoulder and her eyes widened with even more nerves, I realised they must have arrived early. I quickly deposited my meat under the counter and turned round to greet our guests with the detached politeness none of the people here seemed capable of.

'Good morning,' I announced to the group of eight men, four of whom were significantly bulkier than the others, and two women that had entered, juggling suitcases, garment bags, something that looked like a hat box, and a whole bunch of other... stuff. 'Welcome to the—'

'This is ridiculous.' One of the leaner men stepped forward. 'Where are the porters?'

'I...' How would I finish the sentence? We were a small country hotel; there were no porters.

A tall Chinese-looking man with flowing, blond hair and a friendly face appeared next to the flustered older man. 'Don't worry about it, Guy. We'll take care of the bags. Go enjoy yourself.'

The pinched lips and knit eyebrows showed considerable doubt about the amount of enjoyment possible in Saint-Maurice. His desperation to leave won out, though, and he turned his back to me, speaking in hushed tones to the other men. One of the women tried to listen in; the other studied her nails while tapping the floor with her white stiletto. Apparently, they reached a satisfactory conclusion, because Guy imparted a few last wisdoms to the blond man, squeezing his shoulder for emphasis. Then half the party scuttled out the door again, leaving only the tall men. One of them, a dark-haired, bearded man, watched them go but hurried after them as soon as they were outside.

The blond man came up to the reception desk, and from the corner of my eye, I saw our village guests all glued to their chairs, open-mouthed as if they'd never seen people arrive at a hotel before.

'Sorry about that,' the blond man began. 'I'm—'

'Ken Doo,' Jeanette finished breathlessly for him.

He laughed, clearly used to being recognised. 'What gave me away?' He leaned in confidentially. 'It's the hair, isn't it?'

He was joined by an even taller but slightly less bulky man with brown, curly hair, who I pegged as British as soon as he opened his mouth. 'Reservation for Egg, Hjerson, Rice, and Doo,' he demanded in private-school tones. 'And leave out the egg-fried-rice jokes, we've heard them all.'

'Of course,' Jeanette replied, tapping away on the computer.

'They're not staying?' I asked, craning my neck towards the door where the posse had disappeared.

'We all preferred it that way,' Ken replied. 'We'll have some peace, and they'll go back to Lyon where they'll have something to do.' He made air quotes around those last words.

But before Jeanette could give him his keys, the man called Guy returned to the lobby. 'We have a problem,' he said, clutching his phone to his ear. 'The photographer is ill. Food poisoning, of all things. In France! I said we should give up on the whole thing, but that' – he used a word that made me flinch – 'local tourist woman is holding us to our contract.'

The two men frowned, but before I could say anything, Jeanette broke into a wide grin. 'Oh, but that's not a problem. We have a photographer right here. A good one too.'

My eyes widened, and I tried to gesture to her to stop talking, but Jeanette was on a roll.

'I'm sure she'd be happy to help you.'

Guy fixed me with a piercing look. 'You're a photographer?'

'I...' It seemed that was all I was going to say today.

'She's really good,' Jeanette repeated.

'I'm a vintage-style pin-up photographer,' I finally managed.

'A photographer is a photographer.' Guy waved his hand to dismiss my objection. 'If you're free, you can do our shoots.'

'Well... I am today... But—'

'That's wonderful luck!' Ken said, taking his phone from his pocket. 'What's your name?'

'Julie Belmain.'

He had probably typed me into a search engine because he looked up and gave me such a genuine smile that he almost won me over. 'Wow, you really are good,' he said as he handed the phone to Guy.

At this point the last movie star, who'd been quietly waving at the crowd, came up to them and peered at the phone over Guy's shoulder. 'Are you going to make us look good?' he asked, his Australian accent the first thing I noticed. 'I keep my saucy smiles for private use.'

'I always make people look good,' I said, slightly offended. The saucy smile I got in return did nothing to soften that pique.

'You're hired,' Guy said. 'My secretary will call you with the details.' He stormed out of the hotel lobby, leaving behind two smiling stars, and one looking haughty.

'Our keys, if you please,' he demanded in the same arrogant tone as before.

Jeanette handed over four key cards just as the bearded movie star came in through the front door. When all of them had retired to their rooms, carrying their own suitcases this time, I turned to Jeanette.

'Thanks,' I said, scowling.

'What? I thought you'd be pleased.'

'I don't do movie star portraits. I photograph *women* for a reason! I don't even know what they expect of me.'

She had the good grace to blush but didn't give in all the way. 'You could have said no.'

Part of my anger was directed at myself for that very reason, but it was easier to blame her. 'That would have made you look bad.'

She shrugged, and I turned to nod at the last people leaving the lobby now that the movie stars had retreated to their rooms.

Grabbing my meat, I took a breath. 'You said there was a problem with the oven. Why don't you show me that. We'll forget about the photo shoot for now. I'll see what it is they want. Maybe it's just a few shots and I can fit them in whenever.'

3

Tell me you're single

Jacqueline Gavel cursed her feelings for the third time that day. Ordinarily, she had everything in her life well under control, but ever since she heard Ken Doo would be back, she'd done nothing but reminisce. At twenty-five, he'd been so full of life, and plans, and ideals, right when she was losing all of that. He probably didn't even remember her, big film star that he was. She'd been twenty-nine at the time. She was forty-three now.

Life, and plans, and ideals... They were still there, but they weren't as shiny as he'd made them. Jacqueline always tried not to keep an eye out for mentions of him in the gossip magazines. They probably wouldn't tell her the truth anyway. But she wondered if he was still as bright and warm as he used to be before he became famous. She'd picked up bits of information here and there, such as the fact that he wasn't married. It still seemed important somehow, even though it had nothing to do with her.

After he left, life had slowly lost its sparkle. It was as if she was living under an eternal cloud. She'd got used to it. Sometimes that cloud was dark, sometimes it was white, but her life had lost most of its sunshine. She had her work, of course, which was important. She had lovely friends she spent as much time as possible with and she generally didn't feel useless, but there wasn't anything special about her life.

And now *he* had come back. Would he remember her? Would he try to find her? Would she want to be found? She'd contemplated driving to Saint-Maurice under the pretence of visiting her friend but had rejected that idea just as often as it came up. What if she did see him, what then? Would she come up to him? Say hello? Would she dare?

She shook her head. Of course she would. She was a police-woman. She stood up to criminals and murderers; of course she would be brave enough to face an old boyfriend. But still...

Jacqueline leaned back in her chair, pressing the palms of her hands to her eyes. Paperwork. She had paperwork to do. That would keep her mind off the film star in the next village over. She opened her eyes and stared at her computer screen, read a few lines, and her thoughts wandered off again. She read the same few lines and thought about Ken. She read the lines *again*, then growled and got up, switching off the computer in the meantime. Maybe a walk would do her good. She could pretend it was for lunch, even though it was only ten thirty.

Naturally, that's when her phone rang. 'Gavel,' she answered with her usual curtness, though she'd already seen it was her friend Julie calling from Saint-Maurice. Her heart leaped at the possibility of her friend coming into contact with Ken Doo. Would Julie have seen him? Would she have met him? What would she have thought of him?

Not that it mattered. Jacqueline probably wouldn't even see him herself, so why would she care about Julie's opinion of him? She didn't. This was probably about something completely different.

'Jacqueline...'

The hesitation in Julie's voice filled Jacqueline with dread. Though she liked Julie, the woman had a knack for getting into trouble.

'I know this isn't your job, really, but could you come over and have a look at my hotel window?'

'Your hotel window? Why? Has it been smashed? Or is it just that you have a good window display that I have to see?'

'Well... There's a display of sorts. My window has been... besmirched.'

Jacqueline rolled her eyes. 'Your window is dirty, and you want me to have a look at it?'

'Well, it's the way it's been... soiled.' Julie breathed in through her teeth, obviously not sure how to describe her problem.

Sighing, she left her office. 'All right, I was on my break anyway. I will be right over.'

Would she have time to pick up a spot of lunch in the meantime? Julie's window didn't sound very urgent. There was probably time to go get a brie-filled baguette.

However, once she'd bought said baguette, Jacqueline felt too guilty to eat it and placed it on the passenger seat beside her as she pulled out of the parking lot and made for Saint-Maurice.

The whole ten-minute drive, Jacqueline's heart was in her throat. She just happened to see a social media post last night about four movie stars staying at the hotel in Saint-Maurice. And now she was on her way to that exact hotel. The chances of seeing Ken were growing by the minute. What would she do if she saw him? Act natural? Pretend she had forgotten him? Or didn't recognise him?

What would he do in return? If she ignored him, would he be offended? If she smiled at him, would he think she still had feelings he wished she didn't?

Once again, Jacqueline told herself not to be led by feelings. Emotions only got in the way of logic, and she needed her wits about her. With Julie, you never knew. One minute it was a besmirched window; the next, there would be a body hanging from that *dingue* trapeze she'd installed in one of the hotel rooms. Circus theme. Right. Jacqueline hoped Julie was insured. That thing was a death trap. Or an invitation to broken bones at the very least.

Thinking about the hotel had kept her mind from wandering off on tangents such as 'Would Ken be there when she arrived'. But now that she approached the hotel, she saw what Julie had meant when she said the window was besmirched. In big red letters, someone had written GO HOME. They must have been quite quick about it, as the hotel was located on the main square. Though Saint-Maurice was only a small village, the centre of it usually entertained at least a few people frequenting the various shops and businesses. In summer, there were often tourists milling about, taking pictures of the old church and the sun-kissed landscape.

At the moment, though, everyone was gathered around the hotel window, gaping at the big red letters and talking amongst themselves. Jacqueline didn't need to hear them to know what they were saying. *Who could have done such a thing, and for whom was it meant?* She parked in the middle of the square, which wasn't an official parking spot, but she always liked to make use of the perks that come with being a police officer.

As soon as she got out of her car, Julie came running towards her. 'Have you seen it? Can I take it off now?'

'Hold on,' Jacqueline answered. 'Have you taken a picture? And let me take a sample of the paint, just to be sure.'

Taking out her phone, she began procedure, but her brain was already working on the crime. "Go home" could not be meant for someone who lived here, so one of the guests must be the target. Could it be Ken? He did have a history with the area, but why would anyone not want him here? She certainly did.

But she wasn't here for him, or for herself. She had to stay focused on the facts and not be distracted. She was here for Julie and her hotel window, and for whomever the message was meant for.

Having scooped some of the still-wet paint into a little plastic container, she turned to Julie. 'All right, you can clean it now.'

Julie stopped wringing her hands and signalled to one of her employees to start taking down the paint.

'Any idea who they meant?' Jacqueline asked Julie. 'It's all right,' she added when Julie hesitated. 'I know about the actors. Do you think it's them?'

Julie sighed. 'I don't know. We do have a few other people staying, but none of them seem... important, if you know what I mean.'

Jacqueline nodded. 'Not worthy of this treatment. Yes, I get what you're saying. Have you asked them about it yet?'

'No, they've only just checked in. I didn't want to bother them.'

'Half the village is out here. Wouldn't they have noticed?'

'I think they're probably used to crowds. Half the village was in there' – Julie gestured at the lobby – 'when they arrived.'

That made sense. Apart from Julie's forays into crime-solving, the most exciting thing that happened in Saint-Maurice was usually the gossip. The arrival of famous film stars would stir life into the village. 'Have you spoken to any of the other guests?'

'Jeanette is doing the rounds, but most of our guests will have started their days by now.'

'Is she talking to the actors?'

'No, I told her not to, so they could get settled in.'

'We'll have to talk to them at some point. No time like the present. Are you coming?' Jacqueline was already halfway up the stairs and Julie hurried after her. Not leaving any time for her thoughts to turn personal again, Jacqueline got the room numbers from Julie and knocked on the first door. But her heart still leapt when she heard a familiar voice from inside.

'Coming!'

The door opened and Ken's smiling face appeared. Though his smile faltered when he recognised her, it only widened afterwards. 'Jacqueline, I didn't expect you here so soon. Or at all, really.'

She couldn't very well pretend she didn't recognise him then, but she had to remain professional. 'Ken,' she said curtly, ignoring Julie, whose surprised eyes flicked between her and Ken. 'I'm afraid I'm here in a professional capacity. Someone has written "go home" in red paint on the hotel window. Could that mean you or any of your colleagues?'

Ken's smile really disappeared at that. 'No... At least, I don't think so. As far as I know, I'm the only one who knows anyone around here, but I couldn't think of anyone who would want me to go home. Perhaps they don't like the upset to the village? We don't intend to cause any trouble, but people do tend to behave differently around us.'

Jacqueline nodded once. 'All right, get unpacked. I have to ask your friends.'

'Hang on, I'll go with you,' Ken said, closing the door behind him. He knocked on the door next to his. 'Will?'

'What is it?' came a voice from inside. 'Just come in, okay?'

Jacqueline had to make an effort not to wrinkle her nose. Will had been the reason Ken had come to France all those years ago, but that was the only merit Jacqueline had ever found in the man.

Ken opened the door but remained outside with Jacqueline and Julie.

'What?' Will said, turning from where he was draping a coat over the trapeze. His dark eyes looked at each of them in turn. 'Something wrong?'

Jacqueline took over from Ken. 'Someone wrote "go home" on the hotel window. Do you think it could be anything to do with you?'

Will straightened slowly. 'Go home? We only just got here. Who even knows we're here?'

'Everyone, as always,' Ken answered.

'I thought we were coming here for the peace and quiet.'

'And I thought that's what you did not want.' Ken crossed his arms.

'Do you know of anyone who would want you out of here?' Jacqueline interrupted before this could turn into what sounded like an argument they'd had before.

'No, dear lady, I do not,' Will answered. 'And who are you?'

'Will, you remember Jacqueline.' Ken's voice carried reproach but also the hint of a question.

'Oh, yes...' Will drawled the words, but Jacqueline detected no change in his expression. Either he'd recognised her already and asked who she was just to let her know she was unimportant, or he'd forgotten her completely, also indicating how unimportant she was.

She remembered him all right. He'd come here with Ken on a summer holiday, complaining all the while about the heat, the food, the people, and anything else he could think of. It looked like he hadn't changed much in fifteen years.

Jacqueline half turned. 'I will have to ask the others. In the meantime, if you think of something, do give me a call.' She handed Will her card before leaving the room and crossing the hallway to knock on the door opposite.

'Not now, Egg,' a voice from behind the door said. 'I'm just putting away my jimjams.'

'It's Ken – the police are here.'

That got the door open.

'For me? I haven't done anything wrong.' The tall man with the brown curls had appeared in photos with Ken, but Jacqueline couldn't quite remember his name. Ben Something-or-other.

'Someone left us a welcome message,' Ken explained.

'We don't know if the message was meant for you,' Jacqueline hastened to say. 'But we're hoping one of you may be able to tell us more about it.'

'What was the message?' the tall Brit asked.

'Someone wrote "go home" on the hotel front window.' Sometimes the repetitiveness of her job got to Jacqueline.

'Go home? But we've just arrived. That doesn't make sense.' He shook his curls in a dismissal of the whole thing.

'And that's why the police are here.' Ken put his hands on his hips. 'You don't know anyone here either, do you?'

'Never been here in my life. It's only my second time in France to begin with. And my wife's French. Shows you how much I love the country.'

Did it? It would take someone smarter than Jacqueline to work out if he in fact did or did not love France if his wife was

French but he had only been here once before. 'Does she have friends or family in the area?'

'She's from Parree. Meaning no.'

Apparently, people from Paris couldn't possibly have friends or family outside Paris. Now there were two of Ken's friends Jacqueline couldn't stand. But he'd always had a tendency to see the best in people, whereas she was a realist.

'What's going on out here?' a friendly voice asked in an Australian accent. 'Some of us are trying to sleep.'

'No, you weren't.' Will, who had joined the others in the corridor, stepped towards the man who had just opened his own room door. 'Hey, Monty, do you know anyone here? Anyone who doesn't want you here?'

'Here, as in France? Or here, as in this hotel?'

'Someone wrote "go home" on the hotel window,' Jacqueline explained again. This song was getting old.

The man called Monty shrugged.

'Look, none of us know anyone who wouldn't want us here. In fact, there are probably loads of people who do actually like us here. So off you pop.' The Brit retreated and slammed the door in all of their faces.

Jacqueline frowned but put her hand on Julie's arm as she saw Julie take a deep breath to tell that man exactly what she thought of him. Since he was a guest in her hotel, that would not be helpful. Julie had a lot to learn about running a hospitable place. Not that Jacqueline knew anything about it either, but she knew her friend well enough to keep her hand on Julie's arm.

Will shrugged too and went back to his room. Monty asked if there was anything he could do before he, too, retreated behind his closed door.

Julie was still glaring at the Brit's door. 'I hope Jeanette had better luck than we did.' She turned and went back down the stairs, leaving Jacqueline alone with Ken Doo.

Ken put his hands in his pockets and stared at his shoes. Jacqueline looked around at the doors before she could look at him. She was remembering the very last thing they told each other, and apparently Ken was too because he asked, 'So, have you found someone?'

She shrugged. 'Not really. You?'

He looked her in the eye for a long second. 'No one better.'

He moved a little closer, and Jacqueline discovered her body still knew how to produce butterflies.

'Tell me you're single.'

'I am,' she breathed.

'Tell me I can kiss you.' Words he'd said so long ago.

She still knew how to answer. 'Those are dangerous words, Mr Doo.'

She knew what was coming too.

'So arrest me.'

Her small smile grew and she stepped closer, but her phone put a stop to whatever could have come next.

4

Let me guess, you found a body?

Still grumbling about the rude behaviour of tourists and how I was a silent partner for a reason, I joined Jeanette at the reception desk. 'I can't believe you've chosen to deal with this every single day.'

'Oh, had one of those, did you?' Jeanette showed her sympathetic smile. 'Most of them are quite nice, really. They come in expecting to have fun, so they're all excited. But yeah, some treat you like you're a slave. Fortunately, they're a minority.'

'Were the other guests all right?' If they had nothing to do with the painted message, they might have been shocked to hear about it. On the other hand, if the message *was* intended for them, they might not have been shocked but they also likely weren't thrilled.

'Like I said, most of them had already gone out to explore the area, and the few who remained seemed okay,' Jeanette reassured me. 'I mean, they were surprised but not upset enough to make me think it was meant for them.'

'No, neither were the movie stars.' I worried my bottom lip. Someone in the village was angry enough with one of our guests to take out a pot of red paint and defile our window. Wouldn't the intended target know if someone was that angry with them? It didn't seem like an act someone would do out of the blue. Which meant that one of the guests was lying. And some of them were professional liars. I bet it was that rude Brit. The tall one, not the bearded one. I was angry with him already, and I'd only been around him for a grand total of about three minutes.

Now that the paint was gone, at least the crowd outside was dispersing. Among the people left, I spotted Catherine, Tiana's neighbour, and waved at her. Catherine jumped, looked left and right, then lifted her hand in a short and decidedly un-Catherine-like wave. She scuttled off, and I frowned.

'What's wrong with everyone today? Seems the whole world is going mad.' Like what was up with Jacqueline knowing a famous person from another continent and never mentioning that juicy little titbit?

'Catherine doesn't strike me as one of those people who would let her life be changed in any way by a bunch of Hollywood people,' Jeanette said, only half paying attention as she was looking up something on her computer. She tapped away for a few minutes, then resumed, 'Nope, other than our famous guests, none of the people staying in our hotel come up in a search. Unless any of them have something dodgy going on internationally, the actors are the most likely targets.'

'I knew this was a bad idea,' I groaned. The presence of the movie stars could make or break our reputation, even though we were just a small country hotel, and with this message, we were hurtling towards break. I hadn't dared open the internet to see what people were saying about the hotel in all this.

Jeanette let her hands rest on the keyboard. 'I'm sorry, Julie, but it had nothing to do with you. You're a silent partner, remember?'

'I know,' I said through gritted teeth. 'So why am I here?'

Jeanette laughed. 'You wanted to be here! You said, and I quote, "Something is bound to go wrong, and I need to be there." So here you are.'

'And I was right, wasn't I? Something went wrong and here I am. Yay me.' I wasn't going to let her have the last word.

Jeanette shrugged. 'I'm not worried. You'll figure it out.'

'Me?' I clapped a dramatic hand over my bosom. 'I called in Jacqueline for this. It's got nothing to do with me.'

'It's your hotel.'

'No, it's *your* hotel.'

'All right, it's *our* hotel. It's still got something to do with you.'

'I...' I *had* to stop saying that. But I lost my train of thought when I glanced out the window. '*Now* what is it?'

From the side of the *pétanque* court, a patch of level, gravelly terrain where our village's team played every Saturday morning, Sophia, my onetime friend from school, came running across the square towards the hotel. When she came closer, I could see that all colour had left her face and her eyes were wide.

I exchanged a glance with Jeanette. 'Looks like I'm going to have to call Jacqueline again.'

'How does this keep happening to you?' Jeanette looked me up and down as if she could find something on my body that attracted trouble.

'Let's hear Sophia first. It might not be... that.' I didn't really believe my own words, though. I'd been in contact with enough murders now that I knew what people looked like when they'd seen a dead body.

'It's... It's Lutz,' Sophia panted. 'He's dead. Down on the *pétanque* court. It's horrible. His face is all...' Her body shook as she covered her face with her hands.

Jeanette rounded the reception desk and put her arms around the crying woman as she led her to one of the comfortable chairs in the lounge. Lutz was dead? I'd only just seen him. He'd been sitting on that bench at the top of the steep slope leading down to the *pétanque* court. Had he died and fallen down? Or was there something more sinister going on?

I winced as I dialled Jacqueline's number. She was only upstairs so I could have gone up to collect her, but I didn't know if she'd gone into one of the rooms. She did seem to have some sort of connection with one of those guys. That was intriguing in itself. But right now, there were more pressing matters. I braced myself for the eye-rolls and the sighing that our friendship was turning more and more into a professional relationship.

'*Quoi?*'

Did she sound even more short than usual? 'You're not going to believe this,' I started.

'Let me guess, you found a body?'

'How did you know? Well, not me personally.'

'I'll be right down,' was the flat response.

I'd hardly put my phone down before I heard Jacqueline come down the stairs.

'Where?' Oh my, that was some thundercloud hanging over her head, even for Jacqueline.

'On the *pétanque* court.' I pointed through the front window.

'Who is it?'

'Man named Louis Lutz.'

'Did you know him?'

'Not really.'

'She the one who found him?' Jacqueline inclined her head towards where Sophia was being comforted by Jeanette.

I nodded.

'Right, keep her here, I'll be back to talk to her later. And you, stay here.' She emphasised her words with a straight index finger pointing at the floor.

What did she need to add that for? I had no desire to see a dead body. I'd been fortunate enough, even though I'd been involved in several murder cases now, never to actually encounter the deceased myself. I wasn't about to start now. As usual, this had nothing to do with me. I'd be happy to stay far away from it, *as she should know*.

I watched Jacqueline storm out of the hotel towards the *pétanque* court and joined Jeanette to see if I could be of assistance to Sophia, who had stopped crying but was still sniffling. The fact that she'd come running to the hotel and not any of the other shops made me feel responsible for her in some way.

'Oh, Julie, it was horrible,' she now said. For a moment, gone was the Perfect School Mum. In her place was the girl I'd skipped school with to hide out in an abandoned *cadole*, the little huts the winegrowers use to store things or eat in the shade. But after a deep breath, the girl was lost to me once more. 'I didn't think your window was all that interesting, so I returned to the *pétanque* court where I was supposed to meet my team for practice. And then... And then there he was, lying face down in the dust. I turned him over to see if I could help him, and his face was all bloody...' She burst into tears again.

I took Jeanette's place in rubbing Sophia's shoulders so she could get the distraught woman a drink.

'The police are already on their way,' I tried to comfort Sophia. 'They'll find out what happened. Did you know him?'

Sophia snapped upright. 'No! Well, yes. Kind of. I mean, I knew him as that guy, you know, the way everyone knows him.'

Since I didn't really know him, I wasn't sure what she meant. 'How long has he been here? He wasn't here when we were little.'

'No, he came here, I don't know, a few years ago. He is local, but from Ain, you know, the other side of the Saône River? That part of Villefranche, I think.'

'Hmm.' I nodded. Though there was only a river between the two parts of Villefranche, the other side was different. The Saône Valley began on the other side of the river, and the people from Ain lived on a flat surface, meaning some Beaujolais people literally looked down on them. By moving from Ain to Saint-Maurice, Louis Lutz had literally gone up in the world, but whether he would have been welcomed, I wasn't so sure.

And now he was dead. A very undignified way to die, having your face bashed in on the *pétanque* court. Another act of hostility. Even hatred. Could the two be linked? Could Louis Lutz have been the one to paint the letters on the window? He was there on the square before... But I hadn't seen any paint with him.

Conversely, could the message have been meant for him? If he was from Ain, "go home" made sense in a way. But to send him a message on the window of a hotel where he didn't stay? And then kill him two seconds later? Seemed illogical. But then, when was murder ever logical?

Sophia had mostly recovered when Jacqueline's right-hand man, Marc Froment, came in, looking every bit the grumpy cop he always was. He made a beeline for us, nodding his acknowledgement of my existence, then turning to Sophia. 'I'm Brigadier-Chef Marc Froment. You are the one who found the body?'

Sophia sniffle-nodded.

'Can I have your name, please?'

'Sophia Labouche.'

'And can you tell me what happened?'

Sophia repeated the story as she had told it to me.

'So this was after the message had appeared on the hotel window?' Marc asked.

Sophia nodded again.

'And who were you meeting on the *pétanque* court?'

Sophia gave the names of the rest of the *pétanque* team. 'We always practice on a Wednesday, so we were supposed to meet at ten. But because everyone was still looking at the hotel window, we were already late, and I was eager to get going, so I left before any of the others. Now I wish I'd stayed. We're not playing anyway.'

Marc made a note on his tablet. 'Did you know the deceased?'

This time Sophia had had some time to think about her answer. 'Only from passing him in the village. He was quite distinct looking.'

'Was there anything else you noticed? Someone who was there who shouldn't have been, maybe?'

Staring at my knees in front of her, Sophia thought about that for a second. 'I don't think so.'

Marc gave her his card. 'Let me know if you do remember something later. Will you be all right? Do you have someone to take care of you?'

Again, Sophia nodded as she pulled her phone out of her purse. 'I'll call my husband.'

Marc left with a sour look at me. He always treated me as though I'd caused all the murders I'd been involved with. But I was sure he wouldn't be as much against me if he'd been the one to solve them.

Sophia just had time to finish the drink Jeanette had brought her before her husband came to pick her up. But if I thought peace would return to the hotel, I was wrong.

5

Why are you so determined to be a murderer?

'Photo woman!' The arrogant Brit's air gave me physical chills down my spine. He came down the stairs and headed towards the reception desk, where I'd retreated to.

'My name is Julie Belmain,' I said as icily as I could.

He stopped dead in his tracks. 'Belmain? As in...'

'Yes,' I said shortly. I had no idea if he meant the fashion label or my ancient relative at the British court, but whichever it was seemed to have some clout with him, and I was ready to exploit the connection.

He ran a hand over his face, the other propped on his hip. 'Look, I'm sorry about my attitude just now. It's been a jolly strenuous trip. What with... everything.'

I had no idea what he meant. My life was easy. Never anything strenuous. He must have the monopoly on stress.

'Have they caught him yet?'

'Who?' How quickly did he expect Jacqueline to catch this killer?

'The person who wrote on your window, of course.'

'Oh! No, I don't think so.'

'Jolly inefficient. You know, I once played a detective. He would have this solved in an instant.'

'In that case, if you can help, I'm sure the police would welcome your expertise.'

He gave me a look that made me realise the irony of my sarcasm, though he probably knew nothing about my own prior involvement with the police.

Perhaps, though, I shouldn't have judged the man too soon. 'So, what can I do for you?'

'I was just wondering if anyone had explained your role yet.'

I had the feeling he'd actually come down to boss me around, but I liked this new attitude a lot better. '*Franchement*, I was a little surprised, shall we say, to find myself your photographer for the day.'

'Oh, it's not just one day.'

Wait, what? 'What do you mean?'

'No, no, you're supposed to follow us around when we go to visit some of your local festivals.'

'I can't do that! I have other engagements.' Not for another few days, but he didn't need to know that.

At that point, Ken Doo came down the stairs and we both turned towards him.

Oblivious of our conversation, he passed us and went to look out the front window. But since everything was now happening down on the *pétanque* court, there wasn't much to see. The square was empty.

'Looks like it's all over,' he said, turning to us while pointing his thumb towards the window.

I opened my mouth to explain why Jacqueline hadn't returned, but the Brit cut me off, gesturing at me.

'She doesn't have time.'

Ken looked between us and took a deep breath. 'Calm down, Ben. I'm sure we can work something out.'

The other two actors joined us and I felt smaller than ever, looking up at each of them in turn.

The Australian extended his hand to me. 'I didn't catch your name. I'm Montgomery Egg. Call me Monty.'

The name rang a bell. Of course, he was famous, but I wasn't really up to date on the celebrity gossip. I shook his hand. 'Julie Belmain.'

'Good to know you.'

Ben, the haughty Brit, nodded with meaningfully raised eyebrows. That only confused Monty.

'I'm sorry, should I know you?'

'Not unless you're interested in vintage-style pin-up photography.'

'You do pin-ups?' His polite smile turned into a wide grin. 'Are we going to get some ooh-lar-lar?'

The way he pronounced his oh-là-là was terrible, but somehow it made my belly tingle. Maybe there was something to the attraction of these movie stars after all. At least in the case of Monty Egg. If I was to photograph these guys, I'd better remember their names. So this was Monty Egg, the Australian. Then we had Ken Doo, the blond Chinese American. And Ben, the Brit. Who was the other guy again? The bearded Brit? Will. His name was Will. Will what? I needed Tiana here. She could fill me in on everything I didn't know. Maybe I should text her. Would she be awake by now?

I decided to come clean. 'I'm sorry, but you all know much more about what this commission entails than I do.'

'We were supposed to be having a relaxing holiday,' Ben began. 'But when Will joined—'

'Hey, this was not my idea.' Will pushed his chest out like a dark-haired cockerel.

'Will's *agent*,' Ben continued calmly, 'thought it was a good idea to use our holiday as a promotional opportunity. So he reached out to the local tourist board. And before we knew it, we were supposed to have our holiday photographed. Apparently, that was a concession – they had originally asked for a film crew to follow us around.'

'So what am I supposed to photograph you doing?'

Ben pursed his lips. 'Well, I'm here for a garden show.'

Ken raised his hand. 'I'm doing a French pastry course.'

'Books!' Monty said by way of explanation.

Will shrugged. 'I like skydiving. I don't know why I have such boring friends.'

I couldn't help but smile. 'It's almost as if you're only human.'

It made them all chuckle.

'I get the feeling you need more of an introduction than most,' Ken remarked.

I blushed as if Ken had just said 'Get with it, Grandma', but he didn't seem bothered by my ignorance.

'I'm Ken Doo, I play T-Roar, a demigod with an axe to grind.'

'Har har,' Monty commented. 'I play Dark Matador. I'm the bad guy. On screen! I'm not actually a villain.'

'Yeah, you are,' said Will under his breath.

Monty ignored him and pointed to the Brit. 'That's Ben Hjerson. He plays The Defier, but he's not really that smart.'

'I am though,' Ben protested.

Monty pointed to Ken. '*He's* basically a nerd.'

Ken gave me a wave.

'The only one remotely like his character,' Monty continued, pointing to Will, 'is mister straight and narrow over there.'

Will held up his hands Fonzie-style. Since he was wearing a tight, white T-shirt, all that was missing was the ducktail haircut. 'Will Rice.' He shook my hand with something re-sembling a shovel. 'But I also answer to Captain Canon.'

Will Rice took handsome to a new level. A level where, in my view, he wasn't actually that handsome any more because he looked like a cartoon of a handsome man. His eyes were too steely, his jaw too powerful. His nose was too straight and his eyebrows too thick. In other words, he was too perfect. I could see why Tiana was fawning over him.

'So all I need to do is come with you to watch you read, and bake, and garden.' I pointed at Monty, Ken, and Ben in turn as I said it.

'Basically,' Will said.

I breathed out. 'Good. I thought there'd be capes involved.'

They all laughed.

'No. Parachutes, maybe.'

My eyes widened at Will's remark, and I felt a little dizzy, sure all the blood had drained from both my face and the rest of my head.

'No, no, don't worry.' He grabbed my arm when he saw my reaction. 'You can stay on the ground.'

I swallowed, feeling like I'd had a narrow escape. If he'd really wanted me to go skydiving with him, then I might have had to promote Beau to photographer for the day. But would I trust Beau with one of my cameras, falling from a plane? My hands shook just thinking about it.

I wanted to ask for more details but could hardly hear myself over the din that erupted on the square, just outside the hotel. I looked for another member of staff, but they were either busy with lunch preparations or had sneaked off to join the crowd of disaster tourists on the *pétanque* court. I excused myself from the group of actors and pushed through the revolving doors to see what all the racket was about.

'But I killed him! They should arrest me!' Though I couldn't see her in the throng, Isabelle's voice wailed across the square. Some of the people around her murmured answers, but as I approached, I only picked up what the hairdresser said.

'I think you should trust the police.'

Isabelle scoffed. 'What do they know? You saw his reaction when I stabbed him. He turned all purple and white. I don't know how he ended up on the *pétanque* court, but I do know that silly policewoman is wrong. I'm to blame.'

'It sounds as though you want to spend some time in jail,' I couldn't help remarking.

Isabelle pivoted sharply to face me. 'You were there. Did I, or did I not, stab Louis Lutz?'

Why was Isabelle so eager to take the blame for Lutz's death? From her earlier words about him, I'd gathered he'd clearly wronged her in some way, so she might have a motive for wanting him hurt, but if she thought her baguette sword had killed him, I couldn't very well support her in that.

'I saw you poke him with some bread.'

'He clutched his heart! I must have brought on a heart attack that killed him.'

'All he did was rub his belly.' So maybe I was playing things down, but Isabelle must know Lutz's death couldn't be her fault. 'Besides, he was lounging on the bench above the court after he left your shop. He was alive and rude when I passed him later.'

'Delayed reaction.' Isabelle dug her heels in.

Most of the bystanders had shrugged and left by now, but two of the local women had stayed.

'Why are you so determined to be a murderer?' one of them now asked. I was wondering the same.

'Besides,' the other chimed in, 'he had his face bashed in. You didn't do that, did ya?'

Their verdict delivered, they nodded at each other and left.

'He could have got that on his way down the hill,' Isabelle muttered, but she sounded less convinced now.

Though I didn't like the resident gossip much, her downcast manner made me feel for her right then. Was she just seeking attention? Making believe she'd killed a man seemed an odd way of going about it.

'What do the police say happened?' If Isabelle was ready to confess, Jacqueline must have had a good reason not to arrest her.

Isabelle huffed and threw up a hand. 'They say it's an accident. That he was sitting on the bench and must simply have fallen when he got up.'

I glanced over at the bench. 'It's not that close to the edge of the hill, though? The descent is quite steep, but I wouldn't have thought anyone would slide all the way down.'

'That's what Bella said. But *they* think, because of his size...' She moved both hands in a tumbling motion. 'I suppose he could have hit his face on one of the rocks.'

Bella Dudevant. Of course she had been right there, giving her opinion to anyone who would listen. And if she felt someone had recently wronged her, she'd be sure to put their name at the top of the list of her suspicions, whether they had means, motive, or opportunity, or not. Needless to say, I couldn't stand the woman. Even the fact that she'd made the same remark I had made me want to swallow my words.

I glanced towards the bench, calling up an image of the slope and trying to remember if there were many sharp rocks sticking out. 'But you don't think so.'

She shrugged. 'What do I know? I need to get back to the shop.'

She turned and stalked off before I could squeeze any more information from her, but it was probably for the best – I needed to get back to my own duties. I had a decision to make on whether to take this photography assignment. Through the

big, now squeaky-clean window, I could see the group of famous friends laughing and joking around. Two giggly teenage
girls came up from the *pétanque* court and hung around at a
safe distance to ogle them.

Shaking my head, I returned to the hotel. Perhaps this wasn't
such a bad assignment after all. Now that they were settled in,
and no one was asking them if they had any enemies, they all
seemed quite *sympa*, really. Even Ben. But four days of hanging
out with them and taking pictures? While I *should* be trying to
figure out who disgraced my window and put my reputation
on the line? It could have nothing to do with them. Perhaps
the message was actually meant for Louis Lutz. And if so, then
I didn't have to worry about either one. Here was finally a
murder – or was it even that? – that really didn't have anything
to do with me! I did not need to get involved.

Therefore, I *could* easily take a few days and help these guys
out. It certainly wasn't a great business decision, since I would
probably be paid much less than I got from my regular ses-
sions. And I couldn't even use the material for promotional
purposes, since the photos I'd take of them wouldn't be the
style I wanted to advertise. But if I were honest with myself...
it sounded like fun. When was the last time I'd had some fun
with candid shots? And the work itself would be relaxing, since
there wouldn't be any awkward posing involved.

That did it. I went up to the four friends. 'So who's up first?'

6
Tell me what I need to know

'So now I have to be at the airport at two,' I explained to Tiana, who was still rubbing the grit from her eyes. As it turned out, most of the actors' plans were for the coming mornings, which should leave me free for the client I had coming in the afternoon the following day.

'You're so lucky.' She didn't sound particularly happy for me.

'I'm not sure that I am. I don't know anything about these guys. Help me out here.'

'Can't I come with you?'

I made a face. 'I'm supposed to be a professional. What would it look like if I had my fan girl best friend in tow?'

'Like you were the bestest friend this fan girl has ever had!'

'No.'

She pouted, but that only had the opposite of the desired effect on me.

'Really, no.'

Tiana finally relented, though the effort left her even grumpier than she'd been when I woke her up.

'Now, do I have to do a Google search, or can you tell me what I need to know? Start with Will.'

She rolled her eyes but leaned in, as I knew she would. 'Okay, you know he plays Captain Canon, right? And, I mean, he is just so perfect for that role. It's hard to imagine he only had very small parts prior to this one, because he's so gorgeous! Anyway, I don't agree with those people who say he can only play one type of person. It's simply that he's never been given much of a chance. But he is just so nice. Everyone says he's a dream to work with, and he does all this charity work...'

Tiana's eyes turned glossy as she drifted into some kind of daydream.

'And his French is perfect,' I added to the pile of compliments Tiana had already created.

'Isn't it, though? He spent a lot of time in France, holidaying when he was a child with his family, and later in college, though he went to college in the US. That's where he met Ken Doo.'

At the mention of Ken's name, Tiana returned to reality. 'They've been friends ever since, but Ken found fame much sooner. Not that Will ever begrudged him that. He's only ever supported his friend. Ken has said so himself.'

'So Ken has been a movie star for a while?' I asked.

'Oh yes, he's done loads of things. Of course, then he didn't have the blond hair, so he didn't stand out that much. But he's done all sorts, from action movies to romances. Even some fantasy film that flopped. But he's been in the public eye for years.'

'And Ken has been to France, too, hasn't he?'

'How did you know that?' Tiana asked, her eyes wide. 'Yes, they went to France together after college, where Ken got his first break in film. Not many people know that, though.'

'It was hard not to notice that he knew Jacqueline.'

Tiana's jaw literally dropped. I thought she was going to fall off the couch, she was that flabbergasted. 'Jacqueline knows Ken Doo? That's incredible! And she never said anything.'

'I know! Can you believe it? She just kept that little delicious fact to herself. But he remembers her all right. Recognised her instantly.' I enjoyed getting this reaction from my friend. Ordinarily, there wasn't much I could tell her that she didn't already know, but being able to spill some unexpected tea about our friend made me doubly savour the moment.

'Really!' Tiana was in full gossip mode now. 'He's never really talked about his time in France, so I assumed it wasn't important, apart from the fact that he got his first break here. This *is* intriguing.'

'Right? So can you tell me anything else about him? I thought maybe he knew her in her official capacity, but he called her Jacqueline. And I don't think people are usually on a first-name basis with their arresting officer – so that's probably not how he met her. Also, she stayed upstairs when I thought we were done. Only realised she wasn't behind me when I reached the bottom of the stairs and turned around to ask for her thoughts on the matter. The only one left in the corridor by then was Ken, so she clearly stayed behind to talk to him.'

'She didn't! So do you think they were friends or... more?'

I shrugged and suppressed a grin. 'Guess we'll find out.'

'Intriguing,' Tiana said again. 'But no, I can't really think of anything else that someone could hold against him. He plays an axe-wielding demigod, but that's not really relevant.'

Ah, that explained the 'har-har' Monty had uttered when Ken had said he was a demigod with an axe to grind. 'So how about the others? There's a Ben and a Monty, right?'

Tiana nodded fervently. 'Yes. Ben Hjerson. He is married to a Frenchwoman. Got a little baby on the way. And Monty Egg. He's done mostly those really sweet romantic films, but his leap into action has widened his audience. And he's now one of Hollywood's favourites. I can't imagine why. He's terrible. I mean, I guess his acting is all right, but he's just not a superhero. I think he tries too hard. He's always being, like, extra cheerful. Doing community work, and promoting the library. He's a literacy ambassador as well, but I don't know why. I know he likes books, but in my opinion, he should stay far away from them. I know his dirty little secret. He's not as perfect as he wants everyone to believe. If you ask me, he's so good at playing the villain because he's really a bad guy. And I mean, really, a bad guy. *Beurk*. Mark my words. He's got some shady background in Australia that he's covered up. I still can't believe they brought him along.'

I raised my eyebrows at her rant. From what I'd seen, Monty fit the first part about being a stand-up citizen perfectly. Tiana seemed convinced of the second part, but I could tell she wasn't going to say any more. She crossed her arms and stuck her nose in the air. Curious. Perhaps I could coax more out of her later.

'Okay, so tell me about Ben,' I said instead.

'Oh, Ben has been around for ages. He's not the most popular of the superheroes and he was never the most remarkable person in the roles he did before. He played a detective, I think. That was not my thing. Too highbrow. But it's what got him noticed. I never really feel he enjoys what he's doing, though. Not like Ken, who loves his job. You can just tell, right? Whether someone's putting all they've got into their work, or they're just going through the motions?'

I summed up this new information in my head. Will was perfect. Ben did not want to be where he was. Monty was a secret villain, and Ken knew Jacqueline. I scrunched up my eyes, trying to make sense of it all, but somehow the actors only ended up like cartoony versions of themselves in my head. 'Can you think of any reason why someone from around here would want any of them to go home?'

Tiana frowned. 'Why would you say that? What happened?'

'Someone left a message on the hotel window, and now we're trying to find out for whom the message was meant. I mean, *I'm* trying to find out. Those guys don't seem too worried about the whole thing, but people don't go writing angry messages on windows to people they only don't like very much, do they? There's real venom there. I did tell Jacqueline, but then straight afterwards, they found a body. And now Jacqueline is dealing with the body.'

Rolling her eyes, Tiana exclaimed, 'Not another one! At the hotel?'

I fiddled with my nails, staring at the carpet to the right of my foot. 'No, on the *pétanque* court. It's not my fault people keep dying around me, you know. I don't even know them. At least, not this one. He has nothing to do with me. But I do want to find out who wrote "go home" on my hotel window. That mystery is mine, and I intend to find the solution.'

Tiana tapped her lip. 'Yes, I can see why you'd want to know, but I can't think of any reason why any of these four would be unwelcome in Saint-Maurice. You'd have to ask them, but I assume you already did that.'

I pursed my lips. '*Évidemment.* That's how Jacqueline encountered Ken. But they all say they've no idea who would tell them to go home. Are you sure this bad stuff Monty is involved in doesn't have anything to do with Saint-Maurice?'

Tiana shook her head and fluttered a hand. 'Oh no, that's something completely different.'

'If you know something the police ought to be aware of...' I started, frowning at her because she should have thought of this herself.

She frowned back. 'Of course I would let them know. Trust me, the one has nothing to do with the other.'

I narrowed my eyes at her, but she really wasn't going to let me in on whatever she knew, so I got up. 'All right, if you think of anything else, please don't keep me in the dark. You never know what might be relevant.'

I got the distinct feeling she was sticking her tongue out at my pedantic back, but I decided not to check on that. I pulled the door closed behind me and petted Banzaï, who came up to me in his happy-old-dog style, wagging his tail. The dog brought his owner to mind; Catherine had given me a less than enthusiastic greeting this morning. That had been out of the ordinary already, and now Tiana was keeping a secret from me. Add to that the message on the window and the man dropping dead on the *pétanque* court, and my day couldn't get any weirder.

I couldn't help feeling it was all related somehow, but the connection was underexposed and blurry. A local man who was generally disliked, Hollywood movie stars that I was supposed to photograph, and "go home" in red paint on my hotel window. What did they have in common? According to Tiana, none of the film stars had any links to the Beaujolais, but she hadn't known about Ken and Jacqueline, so what else didn't she know?

Swinging the little bag with my meat for today's lunch, I quickly descended the wooded path to my house. I'd best get ready for my first assignment. Perhaps the film stars themselves would drop a clue.

7

This is more Will's crowd

'T-Bone!' A short, stocky man with messy, dark hair and twinkly eyes held up his hand to Thibault, which he shook in that ridiculous manly way that includes slapping each other's shoulders. Apparently, this friendship also included nicknames, because Beau answered, *'Souris.'*

The man didn't look particularly mousy to me, but these nicknames usually had some silly origin that everyone had long forgotten.

'Julie, this is Raphaël Labouche. He owns this place.' He gave a sweeping gesture around the airfield, but I assumed he meant the skydiving school and not the airport. 'Rapha, Julie.'

'You're Sophia's husband, aren't you?' I asked, shaking his hand the normal way. Other than that, I didn't know anything about him, but he seemed like a nice guy.

'And you're the big-shot photographer.'

'Hardly big-shot with those guys around.' I inclined my head to the group of film stars who had arrived ahead of us and were checking out the planes and the parachutes.

'Sorry, I didn't take the reservation. Are you going up too?' His expression betrayed some doubt as to my ability.

For one crazy moment of defiance, I wanted to answer yes, but then my senses returned to me, and I shook my head. 'Not today, I don't think.'

'How about you, then?' He punched Beau's shoulder.

'Can't. I'm here for work.'

'Always an excuse.' Raphaël shook his head, grinning, then turned and went over to the actors.

'He's in the Beaujolais Bikers,' Beau explained before I could ask. We'd wandered over to the entrance of hangar thirteen, where my famous clients were drawing a small crowd.

Thinking I should probably start earning the money the woman who called me at lunchtime had promised me, I raised my camera and started clicking away. After a few shots, though, my finger hovered over the shutter release as I zoomed in on the crowd. No doubt about it. Who other than my influencer neighbour Anne-Bonny would combine corduroy flared trousers with satin slippers, a neon yellow crop top under a blouse that looked like it was made of a bin bag, and a floppy ruff?

She elbowed her way to the front, where she pressed herself up to Will Rice and leered seductively into her selfie camera. Whether it was an act or not, Will was all over it. Where the others politely handed out an autograph or smiled for a selfie,

Will made peace signs, winked at cameras, did his Fonzie impression a few more times, and generally seemed to love the limelight. Before their impromptu collaboration could turn into a full-blown photo shoot though, Raphaël whisked him off to prepare for his death drop.

I debated staying behind with the others while Will was getting ready so I wouldn't have to spend the time imagining him plummeting towards the earth, but I would have plenty of time to take shots of them while Will was in the air. As it turned out, though, Will had his head down for most of his prep, so I could only get a few good shots. After a minute or two, I gave up.

While Will continued putting on his gear, I took a minute to ask Raphaël after his wife's well-being.

'Oh, Sophia's all right. Bit of a shock at first, but once she was home, she quickly got over it. You know she's a tough cookie.'

I did know. She was always a sweet girl and a great friend, but with a stubborn streak. Tiana, Sophia, and I had been inseparable all throughout primary school. But where Tiana had been a goody-two-shoes, Sophia had been able to convince me to skip school every now and then. And every time we did, we got caught. And every time we got caught, I was the one in tears, but she remained stoic.

We had such lofty aspirations when we were little. But after secondary school, my father died and I married the first sweet-talker who reminded me a little of him. Tiana did the good girl thing: finished college and got a job. And Sophia married, had two children and a dog, and became part of the Perfect School Mums set.

'She said she'd be perfectly fine and I shouldn't miss this opportunity.'

I nodded. 'It's not every day you have a celebrity jumping from an airplane.'

'Well, he was here before, wasn't he? Didn't I see him around Christmas last year?'

I raised my eyebrows. People would have noticed if there was a celebrity walking around in the Beaujolais. Wouldn't they?

He shrugged before I could comment, and went on, 'Could have been someone else, I guess. But like you said, it isn't every day they are jumping from my planes.'

I inclined my head. 'I saw I'm not the only one toting a camera.'

His gaze flicked to the man in the corner who was also getting ready for a jump. On the table next to him was a helmet with a camera mounted on top. 'Call me psychic, but I predicted you wouldn't be willing to jump from a plane. Not even for what they pay you.'

I kept quiet after that. I wasn't exactly the only one in our village making a lot of money, but the people who knew me from before, especially the ones who knew that my family had always been the ones in the big house, the ones providing the mayors, sometimes thought I hadn't really earned my money. That somehow clients threw money at me because of my family's history. There wasn't much I could say to that, so I left Raphaël to do his job, and I got on with mine. I took a few more shots of Will getting ready, but once he'd boarded the plane, I found myself alone on the runway, blinking at the summer sun.

Feeling a bit left out, I turned to rejoin the others. The doors to hangar thirteen were still wide open, starstruck people now even spilling out. Either Anne-Bonny really had an active following, or those already present had messaged friends to come over. But my attention was drawn to a shadow on the other side of the building.

'Hey,' I greeted Ken, who looked up from his phone when I rounded the corner. 'No one in there looking for you?'

He pushed off from the wall he was leaning against and shot me a big movie star smile that I immediately clocked as fake. Living with a pretty boy had its advantages after all.

'You don't have to pretend with me. If you'd rather be alone, I'll happily leave you in peace.'

What his smile lost in wattage, it gained in sincerity. 'It's not the quantity of the company, but the nature. This is more Will's kind of crowd. He doesn't care if they're loud and all want something. He's happy to give it. I've always preferred a more personal approach.'

I thought of Jacqueline, but didn't want to butt in at the first opportunity. 'You've known Will for quite some time, haven't you?'

'Mm, over twenty years already.'

'Really? So that's from before you were famous?'

He gave a short laugh. 'We've come a long way, him and me. I'd never have made it without him.'

I glanced up at the cloudless, blue sky where Will should appear at any moment now. 'He doesn't strike me as the supportive type.'

That really made him laugh. 'No, no, not that. But if he hadn't pushed me out of my comfort zone, I would have assumed they'd never pick me and stuck to the auditions for smaller roles. He's been a good friend, and still is. This ridiculous hair? He won't even let me tie it up. Says it's my brand now.'

'He won't *let* you?'

The smile left his face as if chased by tigers. He cast a skittish glance left and right before leaning in a little. 'You don't understand. He can be a very persuasive person. In fact, he is a force to be reckoned with.'

My eyes widened. I didn't like Will much, despite Tiana's conviction he was amazing, but I would never have expected him to be such a bully. What else had he pressured Ken to do? Why would Ken put up with that kind of toxic behaviour for so long? Or had I read him wrong, too, and was Ken's character not as strong as I'd thought?

When he caught my astonished expression, Ken burst out laughing. 'No, of course I can do whatever I want, but his ideas have proven to be effective most of the time.'

I had some trouble getting back to reality. He had me completely fooled with that fearful look. I made a mental note to be aware that these people were actors. Not everything they said was necessarily true.

'We were in college together,' Ken continued. 'I wanted to be an actor and Will had no idea what he wanted to do with his life. His family has money and he wanted to travel. I came along for the first leg of the journey, but I liked it so much that I stayed. Or at least...' He looked me in the eye. 'I liked *someone* well enough to stay. I know you must be curious about that.'

I stepped back, held up my hands, and shook my head in a false and probably completely unconvincing show of indifference.

'How long have you known Jacqueline?' he asked.

'She helped me out of trouble about four years ago.'

'Yeah, she's good at that.'

'So how long were you here for?'

'Six months, maybe.' Again, I got the feeling he knew exactly how long it had been, though his nonchalance was still convincing. 'But she made an impression.'

'Did you keep in touch?'

'No, she didn't want that. I'd found a small role in a French film which impressed the right person, so I was off to Hollywood and she didn't want to be in my way. She had her own career, of course, so that was it.'

His story touched my romantic heart, but having just been bitten by the man's acting talent, I wasn't about to fall for his words again. I'd have to somehow get Jacqueline to tell me the other side, but that in itself posed some difficulty. I was her friend, but hardly her best friend. And when it came to her personal life, she was a clam. I'd had to puzzle together most of what I knew from bits and pieces I'd picked up over the years. I think I would have remembered if she'd mentioned knowing this famous movie star. Still, it had been obvious from her reaction when she saw him at the hotel that she knew who he was, and not just from the gossip magazines.

What kind of a person would keep this kind of knowledge from their friends? And also, what kind of a sleuth was I that I'd never even suspected there might be some romantic tragedy in Jacqueline's past? In spite of myself, I'd come to believe over the past few months that I was something of a detective, so this hurt my hobbyist pride.

Then again, maybe I was reading too much into this handful of facts. Had they said anything more than that they knew each other? I'd already discovered I couldn't trust the expression on the handsome face in front of me. And now I'd found that I couldn't trust my friend to tell me important things about herself. All in all, there was a distinct lack of trust here that I did not like.

'Do you remember anyone else from back then?' I asked, immediately regretting the question. What was I doing? I'd only asked to see if I might know the person and could maybe ask them about Jacqueline's personal past. I was treating her life as a mystery to be solved, not as my friend's thoughts and feelings.

But Ken's reaction surprised me. Though he schooled his expression immediately, I was certain I'd caught some alarm in his features. Real alarm, not played for me.

'Not really,' he answered airily. 'I remember the old lady I stayed with at the time, but she would be in her nineties by now.'

'You must have had colleagues, though, if you were working on a film.'

He sniggered. 'I did, but at the time, people I worked with thought they were quite a bit bigger and better than me. I was just the American they needed for the plot. Most of them lived in Paris and considered anyone who did not live in Paris to be a country bumpkin. There was one local girl who was friendly to me, but I can't even remember her name. What I remember mostly from my time here was lots of cheese and having to take long country walks to get rid of said cheese. But to be perfectly honest, the cheese was just an excuse. Does she still like to hike?'

I took it he meant Jacqueline and grinned. 'It's getting her to stop that's the problem. She doesn't have much spare time, but whenever we're out and about, I can barely keep up.'

I remembered the last walk we'd taken together, which had been almost four months ago already. She'd been called away on her day off to investigate a suspicious death. But I suddenly remembered that she'd been uncharacteristically cheerful that morning, which, come to think of it, had been around the same time we'd got the reservation for Ken and his friends. Maybe I was just imagining things, but I really needed to talk to Jacqueline.

8

Au revoir, poupette

'Capitaine Gavel.'

Jacqueline looked up from her computer screen to find her boss standing in front of her. If someone at the station called her by her full title, that usually predicted trouble. 'Commandant?'

'Is there anything to suggest we are looking for a killer in the Lutz case?'

'I think so. Theoretically—'

'You think so, or there's evidence?'

'Sir, his face was bashed in. It could have been caused by the fall, but I think—'

'It's just that we only have one medical examiner working at the moment and your man is literally a big case. If there is no solid evidence of foul play, I'm going to prioritise real victims. Do you have such evidence?'

Wasn't the mutilated face enough? 'Apart from his facial wounds, not as yet.'

'He'll be the first tomorrow, then. As you were.'

He turned and strode off, leaving Jacqueline to frantically search her notes for anything that might give her a more solid case. She was sure Louis Lutz couldn't have fallen down that slope on his own, but she'd let herself be distracted. The smiling face of Ken Doo had preoccupied her thoughts, and now a killer could potentially get a critical head start. This wasn't like her. Focus!

What did she know about her case? Louis Lutz, fifty-four, had been found on the side of the *pétanque* court in Saint-Maurice, at the bottom of a steep slope leading up to the village square, where he'd been seen sitting on a bench shortly before. He seemed to have stumbled and been unable to stop until he'd reached the bottom, but Jacqueline had looked both up and down that hillside, and wasn't convinced a simple stumble would give a person enough momentum to slide down the entire height. Given his roundness, Jacqueline considered if he could have rolled more easily, but a person's first instinct when they fall is to stick out their hands, to some extent negating the shape of their body.

And then there was his face. There were a few rocky outcrops on the slope that he could have hit, but none of them bore traces of blood, which they must have done if they had impacted Lutz's face with the force necessary to cause this much damage to it.

As far as Jacqueline could tell, the rest of Lutz's body only showed minor cuts and scrapes, so the ruined face was a clear indicator of foul play. She pushed off from her desk and hurried to the commandant's office.

'Ah, Gavel. It has come to my attention that you are personally involved in this case.'

Jacqueline blinked. '*Évidemment*, I was there.'

'You know one of the guests staying at the hotel in Saint-Maurice.'

How did he...? 'Someone I hadn't seen in fifteen years.'

'Someone who was seen talking to the dead man days ago in Lyon.'

Ken had spoken with Louis Lutz in Lyon? Jacqueline's brain was trying to make sense of this new information, but it was like slogging through a muddy stream of questions popping up left and right. What could Louis Lutz and Ken Doo possibly have to talk about? How would they even know each other? Who had seen them talking together and knew to inform the police about it now?

'You said you had reason to believe this was a murder case.'

'Yes, that's why I came to see you. His facial injuries cannot have been sustained during his fall. I believe someone smashed his face in and with the force of that blow, he then rolled down the hill.'

'In that case, I'm going to give this case to Dupin and Rouletabille.'

'Sir! There is no need for that. I can be impartial even if my acquaintance knew the deceased.'

'The very fact that you make that a conditional clause tells me that it's probably a better idea to let Dupin and Rouletabille handle this one. Write up your report and hand it over to them. You know, maybe take a few days off.'

Jacqueline's jaw dropped. 'Sir, I must protest. I've given you no cause to doubt my efficiency. I don't need time off.'

'When was the last time you took a break, Capitaine?'

She'd taken a day off here and there, but she didn't think that was what the commandant meant.

'*C'est ça,*' the man said in a dismissive tone, already rifling through the papers on his desk. 'Finish what you were doing and then make HR happy by reducing the amount of leave you've built up.'

Feeling her shoulders sag, Jacqueline hesitated, and the commandant looked up.

'Is there anything else?'

'No, sir.'

She returned to her desk feeling deflated. Had she even convinced him that Lutz had been murdered? She'd better make sure her colleagues wouldn't write it off as easily as he had done. As she typed away on the report, she couldn't help thinking about this case, though. The people she'd talked to all knew the victim, but none of them seemed to like him very much. Still, no one had been able to give her any idea of who might have been the killer.

Whatever weapon they'd used, the perpetrator must have used some considerable force to do that much damage to his face. But though she looked for blood spatter at the top of the hill, she hadn't found any. Then again, the village square was covered with gravelly sand lined by a grass edge where the ground sloped towards the *pétanque* court. And people had gathered on that edge to see what was going on before she had the chance to preserve the crime scene. Let's hope she could impress upon Dupin and Rouletabille the necessity of getting a forensic investigation team down there.

She finished writing and clicked save, leaning back in her chair. Why had the commandant taken this moment to send her away? He'd never mentioned her build-up of holiday time before. On the other hand... A small smile made its way to Jacqueline's face. The arrival of a certain American made this the ideal time to take up all of that time.

A short man with thinning black hair and a pencil moustache approached her desk. 'Looks like we're taking over your accident case.'

'It wasn't an accident, Dupin.'

'Even better, that gives us more of an excuse to talk to the film stars.'

Jacqueline's eyebrows inched together. He couldn't be serious. 'Did you ask for this case?'

He shrugged, a half-smile on his sharp-edged face. 'Not exactly. Let's just say I'm looking out for your health and well-being by alerting the commandant to the fact that you have been working very, very hard.'

Jacqueline stared at him. She'd felt anger rise, but only for half a second. This was such a pathetic reason for her colleague to want to take over her case that all she could feel was pity. Dupin had had it in for her ever since she got the promotion he wanted, but he just wasn't good enough. Which made it even more imperative that he knew what he was dealing with in this case.

'You have a job to do, Dupin. Make sure you do it.' She gave him a few more instructions, half expecting him to brush them off the table. He wasn't a bad cop, ordinarily, but he seemed a little starstruck. And the fact that he'd gone behind her back seriously damaged her opinion of him. Rouletabille, his partner, was very young. A sharp mind, but without the experience sometimes necessary to do a good job. Still, she made sure to try and convince him, too, before she left.

On her way out, she visited HR and while chatting to the middle-aged lady in that office, Jacqueline tried to let go of the case now that it wasn't hers any more, and focused on her upcoming leave.

'It's good to see you finally take off some time, *poupette*,' the HR lady said in a too-familiar tone. 'Do you have any plans? A trip, maybe? The mountains are beautiful this time of year. Or maybe you plan to visit family? I mean, really, whenever I'm off work, I just like to do nothing at all. Just me, my chair and a good book, maybe a nice drink. That's all you need. All right, I can see you're aching to start your holiday, so don't let me keep you. *Au revoir, poupette, à plus.*'

Jacqueline was out the door before the last goodbye died out. Her first stop was her apartment. If she didn't have to work, then she wasn't going to walk around in office clothes. She switched her suit for high-waisted white trousers with a navy stripe, tucked a thin, loose blouse into it, and grabbed wedges, oversized sunnies, and a wide-rimmed, floppy hat.

She glanced in the mirror to see if her make-up needed a touch-up but then she caught her own eye. Her only thought had been to run to Saint-Maurice, but Ken didn't expect her, of course. She'd only seen him this morning and, as far as he knew, she was still working on a murder case. He'd always been adamant about not interfering in her work and he would have made his own plans for his holiday. She hadn't even asked him for his phone number. The only thing she was sure of was that he was happy to see her, too. *No one better*, he'd said. In all these years, she had still been on his mind and come out on top in comparison to any woman he'd met. Though he'd always been a sweet-talker and she was naturally cynical, she couldn't stop the tingle in her stomach.

She glanced around the apartment. If work was out of the question, and she couldn't just run to Ken, what was she going to do with herself for the coming two weeks? Out of habit, she checked her alerts. Ken Doo had been spotted at a nearby air-field. That must be Will's doing. A local reporter named Pascal Gateau had filled an article with all the usual rumours and gossip surrounding Ken and his friends. Jacqueline zoomed in on the picture of Ken with his professional smile on, then clicked the phone off and threw it on the table. She wasn't going to get anywhere by staring at a screen.

It was probably a good idea to finally decide where she actually wanted to go with this, with him. Fifteen years ago, he'd been a complete surprise to her system. Unlike all other aspects of her life, there was no order to him. No low-level suspicion of how long a good thing would last. No plans for the future other than to make a living as an actor.

He'd made her see what life could be like if you let go just a little. That if you took an afternoon off for no reason at all, you could either end up with a romantic picnic on a hillside, or with a bike ride through a storm, searching for shelter, all the while laughing your head off.

But fifteen years was a long time. He'd honoured her wishes by not contacting her. She'd had her career to think of, and she'd valued his too much to stand in his way. But how many times had she wished he'd ignored her and reached out? Those afternoons off didn't end up anywhere but a lonely coffee at a café, and so they'd dried up. She'd been sure he must have forgotten her by now, but ever since she found out he'd be coming to Lyon, she'd had to work hard to suppress a giddy expectation of seeing him in surroundings so familiar to her, even if only on TV. And now he'd asked to kiss her! If he hadn't been out at this airfield, she'd have run to the hotel after all.

Julie had had no idea what it had done to Jacqueline's insides when she complained about having to make special arrangements for some famous guests. Jacqueline had been careful not to show any interest in Hollywood, so Julie had felt safe in sharing that particular secret, but Jacqueline's heart had exploded. He was coming here! Maybe not to Villefranche, but to a village she visited on a regular basis. The chances of her actually meeting him had spiked.

She hadn't been able to eat properly for days. But now that she'd seen him, she'd completely lost all appetite. Who could think of food when you were better than all the Hollywood women together? She'd tried to focus on work, because every victim needs justice. That was a mantra she'd lived by all her professional life. But now that she'd been taken off the case and sent on mandatory leave, there was nothing stopping her from thinking about Ken and whether she'd see him again. This morning, she'd had all of two seconds with Ken before Julie called her away. He'd wanted to kiss her, but would he have time for her?

Sighing, she grabbed her phone off the table, flopped on her couch and let herself be distracted by news of the recent gang wars breaking out in Villefranche.

9

He is a she

'But he's so cute. Can't we keep him? I already said I would.'
Thibault was holding the most adorable black Labrador
puppy and trying his own best puppy dog eyes on me.

'You should have consulted me first before making such
promises. My studio is not built for puppies. I have sensitive
equipment in there.' And it's pretty. I wasn't going to say
that, but I wasn't about to let a dog loose in my hard-earned
space, either. Instead, I stuck my nose in the air and blamed
someone else. 'He'll scare Henri.'

Technically, of course, Henri did not live with me; he
lived in the garden. And though my own personal stray cat
had never set foot in my studio, he was my perfect excuse
for the moment.

'But look at him!' He held the little dog up next to his
own pleading face, and I was almost tempted, especially
when the puppy started licking his cheek.

'No, I don't want him slobbering all over my white
leather.'

Though past the age of a sulking teenager, Beau gave a very good impression of one. He slouched on the car seat next to me and clamped the puppy to his chest. 'Well, I can't give him back now. Besides, Monty only gave him to me because he can't take him home with him.'

'And that's what he should have told that dumb fan of his.' I kept my gaze firmly on the road so I wouldn't have to harden my heart against the happy little ball of fluff on Beau's lap trying to catch the ray of sunshine on his leg.

'I guess he didn't want to be rude.'

'You'll have to find someone else to take care of it.'

'But he's much cuter than your unofficial cat. Maybe they'll even get along.'

'Thibault Fouquet, you're not keeping the puppy.'

Beau gave me a pout, but then his face cleared and he straightened in this seat. We'd reached the village square, and I assumed he was going to give the puppy back to Monty. But before I'd even switched off the engine, Beau had exited the car and, still clutching the puppy to his chest, made towards the bakery.

'You can't...' I called after him, but he was already out of earshot.

He positioned himself outside the shop window and held up the little pup. Not half a second later, Céline was at his side, cooing and cuddling the little dog. Before I was able to reach them, I could see Beau hitch his thumb over his shoulder and Céline's face drip with compassion.

I knew it. He was making me the bad guy. When I came within earshot, he was saying, 'So I thought maybe you could, you know, take care of him until I get my own place.'

I stopped in my tracks, a little yellow dust cloud at my feet advancing without me. He was leaving? He hadn't said anything to me!

I forced my feet to start moving again. Why was I shocked? I'd always said his lodging above my studio was temporary, and this wasn't the first time he'd mentioned getting a place of his own. Maybe the dog had catapulted him into making that decision? Or maybe...

Of course! It was just a clever ploy to get her used to the dog, so she wouldn't want to give it up. He wasn't going anywhere just yet.

That realisation immediately irked me. Why wasn't he leaving? He was supposed to be here temporarily, and it was already coming up on ten months that he'd been living at my property.

And yes, I realised I was being unreasonable, both wanting him to stay and to leave, but these were my private thoughts and I could do with them as I liked.

Céline had already taken the puppy from Beau and was flattening it against her cheek.

'Are you sure your father is going to agree with you taking in a dog?' I ventured when I reached them.

'Of course, he's got a soft spot for dogs. We used to have a dog when I was little, but this time I can take care of it myself.'

'You do realise that a puppy takes up a lot of your time?'

She glanced at Beau from the side of her eye. 'I think I can handle it. He'll be my little Frou-Frou, won't you, *mon petit*?'

Beau's wrinkled nose and frown reflected my feelings on that name. 'I'm not giving you this dog if you're going to name it Frou-Frou. He's much too cool to be a Frou-Frou.'

'He is a she, and she will be my Frou-Frou.'

He protested again, but I held up my hand. 'I'll see you later. I have to upload my photos.'

As much as that was true, I changed my plans when a car I recognised pulled up and parked next to mine. Jacqueline got out but was too preoccupied to notice me until I greeted her. She started and wheeled round to me.

'Julie! I was coming to see... you.'

'Of course. Who else would you be seeing in Saint-Maurice? *I* should be in my hotel room because I heard *myself* make dinner reservations.'

She flashed a guilty grin and hurried to the hotel entrance. This was a side of Jacqueline I'd never seen before. I'd never even wondered about its existence. It was oddly exhilarating to see her so hopeful and happy. But at the same time, I hoped she wouldn't end up crushed. Their memories of each other could easily turn out to be much more rosy than reality. But as I'd been invited for said dinner, I was sure I could find out a little bit more then. First, though, I had another visit to make.

The living room I was in could have come straight from a magazine. Perhaps it had. The person Sophia had turned into after college would fit right in with the country-style magazine people. A lot can happen in over eight years, but to transform from a croupier at underground poker events to the perfect school mum, something big would have had to change. Of course, she did get married, but somehow I didn't think dare-devil Raphaël would have been the catalyst for that change.

Sophia had left me here to make us a *tisane*, and I moved to the wall of windows overlooking the back garden. Again, everything looked pristine, from the square-cut box hedges to the bright red shed door to the artfully placed child's tricycle. I kept my garden in pretty good condition since I often used it as a backdrop to my photographs, but this was on another level.

Sophia returned with our drinks, and I took a seat on the sofa.

'So kind of you to look in on me,' she said in that gentle voice that used to fool anyone who didn't know her. 'I really appreciate it.'

I looked my old friend in the eyes and was almost surprised to see she meant what she said. She must have grown into the picture she presented of herself. I gave her a sympathetic smile.

'It must have been awful to find him like that.'

She shivered and rubbed her upper arms. 'It was such a shock. You can't imagine. Things like that just don't happen in my life. I'm the one who makes sure the school clothes are clean, and the floors are mopped, and the cupboards are full. I deal with papier-mâché, and comforting boo-boos, and taxiing. Not... that.'

She wrung her hands in her lap, but I suddenly grinned. 'Do you remember when you put that mannequin head in Maitresse Hélène's desk drawer?'

She blinked at me, but then her eyes widened, and a little bit of the naughty girl she used to be shone through. 'She screamed so hard.' Sophia laughed loudly. 'Was she angry! I almost got expelled.' She was shaking with laughter now. 'You were so scared I was going to tell them it was you who had painted that neck.'

'It made the prank,' I said in a mock-dignified voice.

Sophia wiped tears from her eyes. She took a few deep breaths as she calmed down. 'I needed that. I've been on edge ever since I found him.' She looked at me. 'To laugh, you know. Like we used to.'

Her gaze caught the photo of her children on the side table. 'I was afraid I'd have monsters on my hands. Like the way I used to be. But they're all such good kids.'

With that, the conversation turned one-sided with me politely nodding and smiling at her enthusiasm.

'Yes,' she said thoughtfully, taking another sip of her *tisane*. 'Come September, they'll all be at school. With Raphaël at the skydiving school, I'll have four days to myself again. Might try and find a job. Though I've no idea what I would do.'

'Interior decorator?' I suggested, with a gesture around the room.

She laughed. 'But that's more of a hobby.'

'So was photography for me.'

She gave me a curious look. 'Yes, you've done well out of that. And now you've got a different hobby, it seems – if you call solving crimes a hobby.' She pulled on the hem of her skirt. 'I've been a little jealous of you. Your life sounds both glamorous and adventurous. Things I haven't been in years.'

I burst into a surprised laugh. 'It sounds more adventurous and glamorous than it really is.'

I was trying to lighten the mood, but she was still serious. 'Do you think you'll find out who did that to Monsieur Lutz?'

'I don't see why I should. I'm much more interested in finding out who wrote "go home" on my hotel's window.'

She started. 'Oh yes, there was that too. Who would do such a thing?'

'It may just be someone who thinks the film industry spoils our cultural heritage or whatever. Or it may be meant for one of our other guests.' I tried to ease her worry, though for myself, I didn't believe that. During our renovation of the hotel, Jeanette had reduced the number of rooms to make them bigger, so our hotel only had ten rooms, four of which were occupied by the film stars. We had two other families staying – one with small children and one with younger teens – but both families had laughed at the idea of the message being meant for them. One of those film stars must have a secret.

But though I wanted to find out, so I could hold the person who ruined my window responsible, these people were also my clients, in a way. And discretion should be part of my job as a hotel owner.

'What did the police say about it?' Sophia asked.

'I think they're a bit preoccupied now.' But when I saw a shadow pass over Sophia's face again, I asked about her husband and her friends at the *pétanque* club, and by the time I left, we'd chosen a date to get together over coffee and talk about old times. Though I'd been back in the village of my birth for almost a year now, I was still finding new friends, even if they were old ones. Counting my blessings on a pink cloud, I went home and dressed for dinner.

When I joined the film stars at the hotel, the restaurant was packed. My mother had already told me that she'd given Jeanette a special permit to put more tables out on the village square so she could accommodate the reservations made from Villefranche. People were gaping at my table companions, but the person most uncomfortable with the situation seemed to be Jacqueline.

'Is it always like this?' she whispered to Ken, but it was Ben who answered.

'On our own, we can kind of blend into the background, but when there's more of us together, it's usually chocka like this.'

I narrowed my eyes. If that was true, maybe there was something to what Raphaël had said about seeing Will in the neighbourhood at Christmas. I stole a glance at the beautiful man lazily tearing off a piece of bread. No matter how taken Tiana was with him, I could easily see him hiding some dark secret. Him rather than Monty, who was cheerfully looking around and waving at fans.

'Chocka?' Jacqueline turned a questioning face towards me, but I had no idea what he meant.

'Chock-a-block? Crammed?' Ben said, a little louder than required.

'We tend to make a bit of a public display on the first night to get the gawking out of the way. Once people get used to us being in the hotel, the attention often diminishes,' Monty said, gesturing widely with a glass of red wine that sloshed precariously but never actually spilled.

'Did you get the chance to see any of our local sights?' I asked him.

Ken was the only one who'd returned to the hotel after the skydiving experience – and now I knew why – but the others had ventured into Villefranche, looking to get a taste of the local culture, as Will described it. Judging from his rosy cheeks and the slight slur of his speech, he'd imbibed said culture in sufficient quantities to testify to its exquisite flavour.

'Wine and old buildings,' he declared. 'I know which one I prefer.'

I exchanged a glance with Monty, who sat next to me.

'There's more to the Beaujolais than wine and architecture,' Jacqueline said.

Oblivious to her icy tone, or perhaps deliberately ignoring it, Will continued, 'Sure, sure. There's also those sticky rolls

with the pink stuff in, and those overpriced, green, choco-
latey, sweet things that I can't get enough of.'

Clearly the *coussins*, alcohol-infused local delicacies, had
contributed to his current state. He'd have *une gueule de bois*,
a wooden mouth in the morning.

'Those are good,' admitted Ben. 'If only they'd serve them
with a decent cuppa. You know, I did a *gap yar* in Gay Parree. That's where I met my wife. *Crossonts* everywhere. But
all you get to drink is a thimbleful of liquid coffee beans.'
He shuddered, as I wondered whether I'd lost my ability to
understand English. Ben prodded his steak tartare. 'This is
raw!'

'So, are you coming with us next time?' Monty asked Ken.
'Or is your time better spent?' He wiggled his eyebrows.

Ken cast down his eyes, but before he could answer,
Jacqueline's phone rang.

'I'm sorry, I'd better take this.' She left the table to answer
the call, and Ken's friends pounced on the opportunity.

'So, what happened?' Monty made no effort to hide his curiosity. 'Is she still available? Is she still, you know, interested?'

'Yes,' Ben added. 'And will we now finally hear less about
her? Or will she really be the only thing you can talk about?'

I pressed my lips together to hide a smile, but I was sure my
eyes were twinkling so hard, that smile must show nonetheless.
For all her toughness and self-reliance, Jacqueline could use

some positive influence in her life. And from the glow that emanated from Ken's face, he wanted to audition for that role.

'Yes. And no? Maybe? I don't know. We'll see,' he rambled, but was saved by Jacqueline, who returned with a frown.

'Something wrong?' I asked.

She took a deep breath. 'You know that man who died outside this morning? I've been taken off the case' – she swallowed – 'but the medical examiner didn't know that. He called me to say that the man was not murdered. His spleen burst and he died of internal bleeding.'

'Well, that's good, right?' Monty asked. 'That he wasn't murdered, I mean.'

'Ordinarily, yes, I suppose. But his face was smashed after he had died. Whoever did that used a rounded object, like a large pebble.'

'Or a *pétanque* ball?' Beau asked.

Jacqueline shrugged. 'Perhaps, but we didn't find any at the scene. I'm sure Dupin and Rouletabille will ask to see the players' balls.'

I grimaced. 'Who would do something like that?'

'That's what I'm wondering. But I'm off the case.'

'Why?' Ken asked, suddenly serious.

She gave him a long look that made everyone feel uncomfortable, but Ken nodded. 'I'm impressed with the police work in this country.' He leaned back and stared at the steak tartare. 'I knew him, the dead guy. From when I was here before.'

'Is that why you went to talk to him?' Will asked, making everyone stare at him in turn. 'You can hide your hair under a hat to fool the rest of the world, but I know you. And my room looks out over the square.'

'Why didn't you mention this before?' Jacqueline drilled both Ken and Will with her scary policewoman look.

'I only saw him for a second. The whole thing had nothing to do with me,' Ken said to the steak tartare.

Will held up his hand as if he was being sworn in in court. 'True, I saw you walk away from the fat guy and he was still alive then, because he made a rude gesture behind your back.' He turned, scowling, to Jacqueline. 'And besides, *you're* off the case now, so what do you care?'

'Every victim deserves justice. He may not have been murdered, but his corpse was desecrated. Whoever did that should not be allowed to walk away scot-free.'

'Why did you want to talk to him when you knew him fifteen years ago and he didn't even like you?' Ben suddenly asked. I'd been chewing on the same question. Ken had masterfully changed the subject when I'd asked him if he knew anyone from back then, I now realised. What else had I missed?

'He, erm... knew something and thought he could make me pay to keep that quiet.'

'After fifteen years?'

'Apparently so. But I wouldn't give him the satisfaction. And yes, I know.' He put his hand on the edge of the table near Jacqueline. 'That would have given me a good motive for murder if he had been murdered, but he hasn't. So I'm not a suspect. Now, why are you off the case?'

Jacqueline rolled her eyes. 'They took me off before they knew that. They also asked me to take some time off.'

'Remind me to thank them later.' Ken was already smiling again.

I had one last question, though. Though I could now explain Ken's reaction at the airport when I'd asked if he knew anyone else from back then, not everything was clear. 'Could Lutz have written the message on the window to you?'

He shook his blond mane. 'No, he didn't want me out of here. He just wanted money. Sorry.'

Monty leaned towards me. 'So, you and Beau...'

'No,' Jacqueline answered for me, and Monty gave me a special smile that made me launch into quite the monologue about my boyfriend Léon and all the good work he was doing in America. I hoped the message was clear for when I'd see him again in the morning.

10

There must have been some good in him

My phone rang before my alarm had gone off the next morning. I opened one eye just enough to look at my smartwatch. Madame Dufaux? Why would she be calling me at this ungodly hour? Why did I even have her number and why did she have mine? We knew each other's names and we said *bonjour* when we met each other in the village or anywhere else. But she was not in my inner circle.

'Awwo?' was my intelligent greeting.

'Madame Belmain, I know it's early and I do apologise, but I think you should see this.' All in all, I considered my greeting more polite than hers. 'I'm at Louis Lutz's house. I was his cleaner. Please come quickly.'

She'd rung off before I could answer, and I blinked my other eye open. Now what was I supposed to do? I didn't know where Louis Lutz lived.

I grabbed my phone and texted Madame Dufaux back for the address, adding a second message after some consideration.

Will I need assistance?

Beau wouldn't thank me for that opportunity, but if I found something that he would consider a clue, he'd also give me the evil eye for not including him. Then again, Louis Lutz was not murdered, so there was no investigation and hence no clues. But what else could be so important that Madame Dufaux would call me this early in the morning?

The address came through as I was dragging myself out of bed, along with reply to my question: *I don't think so, unless you mean emotional support.*

Which did nothing to settle my nerves. Assistance it was. My phone rang for ages while I was getting dressed. He was only down the corridor in my guest bedroom while his studio was being fumigated, but I did not want to walk in unannounced.

Eventually, Beau answered. 'Don't tell me there's another grasshopper.'

'No,' I said indignantly, though I couldn't help peeking into the bathroom to be sure. 'We've been summoned.'

'By whom, *le President*?'

'Madame Dufaux.'

I had to call him again, but at least he picked up relatively quickly this time. 'She said I would need emotional support. Now get up and support me.'

'You need professional support,' he grumbled, but I heard the bed springs creak and expected to see him downstairs after I hung up.

The very basics of makeup would have to do for today, but by the time I had my face on, Beau was already drinking coffee.

'This better be good. It's six... thirty.' He swallowed a swear word and I ruffled his hair, which made him even angrier.

'Think of all the possibilities this day could bring now that you see it in a brand new light.'

'If it was winter, there wouldn't even be any light.'

'Good thing it's summer then. Drink up!'

I don't know why his grumpiness always made me extra chipper, but even at six thirty, it had the same effect as always. I skipped to the door, which I could because I was wearing wedge sandals, and waited in the car for the zombie to join me.

'It's only two streets from here.'

'Yes, but up the hill, and it's really early, if you hadn't noticed.' I started the car and drove the half a minute up the hill, where Madame Dufaux's little black car was parked in front of a medium-sized, thoroughly modern house that stood out among those around it that were built in the traditional style with the local yellow stone. Compared to those, Lutz's house, though not unattractive, looked sterile with its white walls and black-cased, large windows with metal shutters.

Madame Dufaux opened the black door and ushered us in. The interior of the house felt just as clinical and clean as the outside, its spartan, black-and-white, glass-and-metal decor only broken up by a very few odd pieces of decoration. There was a misshapen clay ashtray on the coffee table that looked like it had been made by a child; a single painting of a woman hung above the TV; a solitary book graced the top of a filing cabinet. On the other side of the room was a desk that held a serious-looking computer-set-up with bells and whistles I could only guess the function of. Hanging above it was a 'diamond painting' of a pair of gaudily coloured parrots, made from one of those kits that come with a design and a million tiny, shiny beads.

I looked around for anything that could have prompted Madame Dufaux to invite us here, but nothing in the austere living room stood out. Beau had drifted over to the painting above the TV and was regarding it with a frown.

'Not your style?' I asked, but he only hummed, and I turned to Madame Dufaux, who stood by a large, black leather armchair and was all but wringing her hands.

'Monsieur Lutz always said it was a picture of a murderer. I kind of liked it before he said that, but now I can't wait to get rid of it.'

I gave the painting a second glance. It was artfully made, the woman showing a kind of demure kindness but also a hint of pride. She was standing next to a statuette on a pedestal that had a delicate marble pattern but was partly hidden by a plant. I didn't recognise the woman, but from this picture, I wouldn't have thought I was looking at a murderer. Instead, I asked Madame Dufaux, 'So what is it? How can we help?'

'*Alors*... The thing is, I don't know if you know, but I was Monsieur Lutz's cleaner. And though, of course, it won't help him much now, he'd already paid me for the month, so I thought I'd just come in and do what I could to get his affairs in order, or at least the things that I knew could maybe help someone.'

I was afraid this explanation of why she was here could go on for some time, so I said, 'But what does that have to do with me?'

'*Ben*, you see, he had this filing cabinet, and I was never allowed to touch it. But now that he's dead, and I...' She took a deep breath. 'Last night, a man called me to tell me I was going to inherit all of Louis Lutz's things. Apparently, I was the only person he actually knew. But I didn't really want his things, and now that I've seen this, I really don't want them. But I don't know what to do. And when I saw your name, I thought maybe you would have a solution.'

The poor woman was about to have a nervous breakdown, so I made her sit down in the big chair that dwarfed her small frame even more, and asked where exactly she'd seen my name.

'One of the files.' She fluttered her hand in the direction of the filing cabinet. 'It's on the desk.'

Beau had come to squat in front of the chair, and remembering his boast that he was good with nervous women, I left him with Madame Dufaux and went to inspect the file. A manilla folder with my name on it held a few sheets of paper and some photographs. They contained my personal data – my date of birth, address, and such things – as well as information on my business, including an excerpt from the Chamber of Commerce and my price list. But most of the paperwork was on my ex-husband, Franck Fouquet, who had recently been released from prison after a four-year sentence for fraud. None of the information in this file was new – though it wasn't common knowledge or publicly available – but why on earth Louis Lutz would keep a file like this was beyond me.

I glanced at Madame Dufaux, who seemed on the verge of tears.

'He told me he was an IT specialist,' she cried out. 'Said if I kept him in good food, he would reward me handsomely. But just look in the top drawer of his desk. He only ever wanted the bad stuff. Fried chicken, heavy sauces. I told him it would be the death of him. But he just laughed and said someone would make sure he didn't have to worry about that. And now,' she sobbed, 'it looks like someone did.'

'Actually,' I began but held my tongue just in time. I didn't know if it was supposed to be public knowledge that Lutz had died before his face was mutilated. Officially, Jacqueline wasn't even supposed to know. Of course, the ruptured spleen probably had been helped along by the 'bad food' Madame Dufaux had provided, but I wouldn't be telling her that either. 'We can't be sure of that,' I ended instead.

But I did open the top drawer of the little chest under his desk to see what Madame Dufaux had meant. It was full of snacks: chocolate, sweets, protein bars, and an unopened box of *coussins*, the emerald green cardboard standing out among the plastic wrappers.

'There are more files,' Madame Dufaux whispered, swallowing another sob.

Closing the little drawer again, I walked over and opened the top drawer of the filing cabinet.

My fingers ran over the folders inside, each labelled with the name of one of the people from the village. Or at least, the ones I recognised were people from the village. I took out the folder with Tiana's name, thinking there wouldn't be anything in there she wouldn't want me to know. Indeed, everything in the folder was no news to me: age, education, titles of her books, the break from parents. Even her allergy to cockroaches was in here. But the question remained, why did Louis Lutz have files on the villagers in his cabinet?

My eye was drawn to a folder labelled with the name of Charles Cochon, who was the butcher and Isabelle's husband. Did I dare have a look? There could be private information in there, but if I didn't check, how was I ever to find out why I was here and why Lutz had files on people? It was clear from the encounter I'd witnessed in the butcher shop and Isabelle's reaction after his death that there was bad blood between the two of them.

I took the folder out of the drawer and opened it. While my eyes raced over the lines inside, my jaw dropped. Here was evidence of Charles having an affair. There was a number at the bottom of the page that looked like an amount of money, but it had a big red cross next to it. The only conclusion I could draw was that Louis Lutz had tried to blackmail the Cochons, and it had backfired. If Charles had come clean to his wife, both about the affair and about the blackmailing, that explained why Isabelle had been gone for a few weeks, and also why she would have been so angry with Louis yesterday morning. If this had been Louis's game, that also explained why people didn't like him very much.

I lowered the file and stared into space. What was it with this village? This was the second person I'd discovered collecting people's secrets. Granted, the first had never asked for money, but not all secrets were worth that much. So unless Louis really also was an IT consultant, he couldn't have lived off the secrets of people in just this village. I opened the other drawers in the filing cabinet. None of these names looked familiar to me, but it was obvious why – dividers labelled with place names separated groups of files. Some were villages in the Beaujolais area; a number of them were around Lyon and even further away.

'I only looked at two or three,' Madame Dufaux said. 'Enough to know what they were about. I know I have to get rid of them, but I panicked.'

'*Non.*' I turned towards her. 'Thank you for calling me. This should help the police figure out who might have disfigured his face.'

But could that person really have been Isabelle? Was she capable of doing something so brutal to a man after his death? Besides, there were plenty of other names in this cabinet, which must mean plenty of people who wanted Lutz dead.

I was already reaching for my phone when I remembered Jacqueline had been taken off the case, so I closed the cabinet and went over to Madame Dufaux. 'I think you should go home, have a drink, try to relax a little. And once you feel your head is cleared, call the police and show them the files.'

Madame Dufaux nodded.

'You were right in calling me,' I reiterated. 'Those files will help get justice for him, whether he deserved it or not.'

She heaved a sigh and looked up at the diamond painting. 'He wasn't all bad. Look, he made that and he was so proud of it, he hung it above his desk. It's actually a hobby of mine, you know, to do those things. One day he asked me if he could borrow one. See if he could do it. So I gave him one for himself, and he made it, and look what he did. There must have been some good in him.'

I wrapped my arm around her and led her to the door, beckoning to Beau, who was loitering near the desk. He followed us out and closed the door behind him.

'Don't worry about those files,' I told Madame Dufaux. 'The police will come and collect them, and you can enjoy all the other things that Louis has left you. You were there for him when no one else was, so you deserve it.'

She nodded but seemed unconvinced.

'If you like, I can come over when the police come and collect the files, but I do have to go to work now,' I offered, but she shook her head.

'No, that won't be necessary. Thank you, Madame Belmain.' She looked me in the eye. 'Thank you, Julie,' she said with a small smile.

Feeling I'd done my good deed for the day, I got in my car where Beau was already waiting, a manilla folder on his lap.

'What—' I started.

'It's only yours. I thought you might like to keep it.'

'This whole thing is thoroughly weird,' I said, putting on my seat belt. 'It makes going to a gardening festival with a movie star seem almost pedestrian.'

11

Have you been a naughty girl?

Le Festival Botanique took place in a *domaine* close to Pruniers, a village in the vicinity of Villefranche. It was a picture-postcard spot – rolling hills blanketed with vineyards, where almost-ripe fruit basked in the warm sun. Bang in the middle of the estate was a substantial *manoir* in the same seventeenth-century style as my brother's mansion. The building was mostly known for its clock tower, a local curiosity as the clock had a second hand, which is unusual in such a big, outdoor clock. I'd picked up rumours that the estate was in trouble and that was why they hired out the extensive park of formal gardens behind the main building for events such as this.

Today, the gardens were overrun by stalls selling plants, gardening equipment, and all kinds of other, marginally related objects and services, from *plantes rares*, to quirky homemade decorations, to garden furniture. People in sun hats and dark glasses were milling around, trying to focus on the wares on offer and pretending not to be distracted by the tall, handsome man being photographed all the time. They were here for their precious gardens, not for a film star.

Though several of my acquaintances had green fingers, I certainly did not. I paid someone to keep my garden looking like a perfect backdrop for my pictures but hardly ever spent time in it, except when I was with friends or for the occasional quiet night in the garden with Beau, but he usually had better things to do at night. Sometimes I took my calls to Léon outside, but since the Wi-Fi got sketchy out there, I preferred a good connection to my boyfriend to sitting by myself in a dark garden.

My British charge was in his element, though. He darted from stall to stall, rubbing leaves, sniffing flowers, and frowning at decorations that weren't to his taste. I was already clicking away on my camera, focusing mostly on Ben, but every now and then annoying Will by training my camera on him.

Monty had found an excuse not to come. Ken was here, though so was Jacqueline, so I had only seen a glimpse of him. But Will was moping in Ben's trail, poking things that clearly didn't interest him and sighing every time he checked the time on the tower clock. Whenever I directed my camera at him, however, he instantly transformed into the most genial garden lover. He would hold up some trinket or other and study it as though it could change his life. Or he would cup a flower and hold it to his nose in ecstasy. Oh, he knew how to work the camera. Those photos would be worth gold. But we weren't here for him, so I didn't indulge his vanity too much. Pretty soon, the uncurious veneer on the other visitors would wear down, and he'd be inundated with fans asking for selfies anyway.

Ben passed by a table showcasing colourfully painted pebbles. He held his nose high and dawdled at the next table, which sold bonsai trees. Will slouched, sighed again, and picked up one of the pebbles in an attempt to alleviate his boredom.

'*Combien?*' he asked in accentless French without looking at the seller.

'For you, *chéri*, it's free. To remind you of the glorious Beaujolais.'

I knew that voice.

'Bonjour, Catherine,' I said to Tiana's neighbour, who held aloft a red-tipped paintbrush.

She started and only just managed to keep her smile in place. 'Oh, Julie, yes, hi.'

What was up with her? She was always flirty with any handsome man she might meet, so it wasn't as if these handsome men were any different. Not to her or to her boyfriend Daniel, anyways. But then I remembered she'd acted rather strangely the day before, when I met her at the square. Was it me she had a problem with?

Catherine bowed her head over a pebble she was transforming into a ladybird, and when I happened to glance at Will, he was grinning at me, a mischievous glint in his eyes. As we moved away from Catherine, he whispered, 'Have you been a naughty girl? She doesn't seem to like you very much.'

I chose to ignore his angling and lifted my camera in hopes of distracting him, but he put his hand on the lens and forced the camera down.

'Perhaps you're not so perfectly prim as I thought, then. Maybe we could even have some fun.'

Ken's words from the day before came to mind. *He can be a very persuasive person.* I wasn't sure what Will was trying to persuade me to do, but I didn't like it. In fact, there wasn't much about Will that I did like. Still, Ken had at least tolerated him for the past twenty years, so he couldn't be all bad. And Tiana swore to me that he was the best of the bunch. Perhaps I should let her inform me of any good qualities he might have.

I was still thinking of a professional answer, when Catherine's voice sounded over the general hum of people buying plants.

'Oh, le petit chou!'

Behind Will, Céline had shown up with the black Labrador puppy in her arms. Catherine's own yellow Lab lifted his head from where he was lying at her feet but couldn't see what the fuss was all about and went back to sleep. Catherine, however, had thrown down her paintbrush and stretched her hand towards the pup.

Céline, all smiles, handed her the dog, who wagged his tail furiously as soon as he landed in Catherine's arms and started licking her face, making her burst into even more unintelligible cooing.

As adorable as the sight was, though, I wondered where my assistant had got to. If Céline was here, he couldn't be far off. But I couldn't find him anywhere in the crowd. Why was everyone abandoning me?

'Hey, Jules,' said the person I had abandoned. 'Look, I found a friend.'

I turned and had to make an effort not to grimace. Ben had his arm around Anne-Bonny, who was clicking away on her selfie camera. A friend indeed. I had seen her posts last night. Not only was she stealing my angles, but she had captioned her pictures with the question, *Does Julie Belmain have to take other commissions now?* Implying that my business would not support me any more. It had taken all my self-control not to send her my bank statement. I could only hope her circle of influence did not mix with mine, or else rumours like this could ruin my business, and I'd have to start all over again. Of course, I'd done it before. And I was in a better position to do so now. But I'd rather not.

THE GIFT OF DEATH

Thinking of that last time put me in mind of my ex-husband, who had been my downfall four years ago. And suddenly, I remembered seeing Anne-Bonny talking to Franck's right hand man only a few short months ago. At the time, I had chosen to see their meeting as a coincidence, but seeing her here again, when no one was supposed to know the film stars' itinerary, I couldn't help but wonder whether she employed the same tactics as Franck had done, and where she might have learned to spy like that.

Though I'd learned my lesson after Franck and used every precaution available to guard myself against cyber-attacks and fraud, I knew that as long as I was connected to the internet, there was always a chance someone could be spying. And who would suspect an innocent social media influencer like Anne-Bonny in her glitter miniskirt and felt bustier? The giant sunglasses in the shape of sunflowers alone were a perfect disguise. Nobody. No one would suspect her but me.

All this flashed through my mind as I pasted on a fake smile and lifted my camera to capture the evidence of Anne-Bonny's vanity, and I was not above making sure I'd use a most unflattering angle. I'd keep that picture just in case she made another one of those suggestive remarks.

'Have you found something you like yet?' I slipped my arm around Ben's and guided him away from the fashionista in the most casual way I could manage. If he was surprised by my

action, he didn't let on, but I could feel Anne-Bonny staring daggers at my back.

'Oh, plenty,' Ben enthused. 'It's a bit early to be thinking
of Chrimbo presents, even for me. But I might just take one
of those little wooden geese home as a souvenir. They're
rather spiffy. *Excoosay*, can I have *oon*... What's a bird?'

'*Un oiseau.*'

Ben huffed and turned to Will. 'No wonder they all
sound like porn stars – even their counting starts with a
moan.'

I decided to ignore that remark, as I still had part of my
assignment ahead of me. He paid for the goose, and we
continued down the path.

'And what about the...' My voice faltered, and I ended in
a whisper, 'Plants.'

We'd come to a cordoned-off section of the festival that
had warning signs all over it. *Danger, poisonous plants.* Ordinarily, that wouldn't have shaken me so much, but I
recognised one of them. I'd seen one just like it this morning, in a painting in Louis Lutz's house. A picture of a
murderer, Madame Dufaux had said Louis Lutz had called
it. What if he hadn't meant the woman, but the plant?

'Yes, lots.' Ben laughed. 'I'll know where to come when
we visit. On holiday! I mean. It's... a bit cumbersome to
take one on the plane with me. Oh, look.'

He pointed at some shiny wind chimes that I'd seen him snub earlier and wondered why he wanted to distract me from what he'd just said. But fate provided me with a different distraction.

Almost the same moment I noticed her, she noticed me. Apolline Bailly. Active in all the clubs and boards, she and her husband Corentin were held in the highest regard by the mayor of Saint-Maurice – i.e., my mother. I, however, was not 'her kind of people'. I made the right kind of money but not in the right kind of way. Our paths had crossed before and neither of us had enjoyed it.

And here she was again, behind a brand new, bright red table filled with all kinds of little cacti, some fuzzy and cute, and some nasty looking, with big spikes. One of the spiky ones was actually shaped in such a way that it looked like it had a long face, just like Apolline.

Although neither of us were eager to converse, I couldn't very well ignore her without giving her cause to label me as rude.

'Apolline. Good to see you,' I lied.

'And you,' she kept up the ruse. 'I heard someone wasn't too happy with your service at the hotel. So rude.'

I knew this was an attack, but I had to stop and think for a minute what she meant. Then I realised she was turning the message on our front window into an insult.

'Oh, how quaint,' I said with a laugh. 'You're the first person to not immediately realise that the message was meant for one of our guests.'

She said sweetly, 'Well, I suppose you just can't tell what kind of people you will be attracting, can you?'

She knew as well as I did that her husband was among those doing business in our restaurant. Théo's cooking had already been famous among locals, but he'd been a bit of a hidden gem. Now that he had an attractive place in which to display his culinary skills, the restaurant was quickly becoming known to gourmands in a wider area. Foodie websites were picking up on this and bringing in still more customers.

I could easily think of a retort that would include Corentin Bailly in the rabble Apolline had implied came to the hotel. Instead, I slowly raised my eyebrows as I looked down my nose at her. Ordinarily, that would require me to tip my head back quite a bit, as she was tall and I was... not, but she was sitting, and for once, I had the height advantage. I made good use of it. I stared at her until she blinked and looked away, and I had to remove myself from her table so I could smile victoriously without her noticing.

I hadn't gone two steps, however, before two men cut me off. Both were relatively short, one slightly older but with raven black hair and a black moustache, the other younger, with a round face that looked quite red as if he'd been running, but he wasn't out of breath. The two identified themselves to Apolline behind me as police officers.

'Madame Bailly, we are trying to locate your son. Can you tell us his whereabouts?'

'Constantin? I haven't seen him in days.'

My ears perked up. Apolline's son only ever came to Saint-Maurice to ask his parents for more money, and I'd seen his motorcycle in the village only yesterday. He'd been getting into trouble since he was a young teenager, but to his mother, he was still the perfect little boy. Why would she lie about having seen him?

'Why are you looking for him? Is something wrong?' I heard her ask.

'It's in relation to the death of a Louis Lutz. We have information that your son was familiar with the deceased.'

I'd turned around by now and was gawking along with every other person who happened to be in earshot, so I could see Apolline pale at the mention of Louis. Suddenly, I wished I had taken a closer look at the files in Lutz's cabinet. Had there been one for Apolline? Or maybe her son? Oh! Could the message on my window have been meant for him? But no, that made no sense. I was starting to make those two stupid words, "go home", rule my thoughts. Why would anyone write a message for a villager's son on the hotel window? Unless...

Good thing I wasn't a curious person, or I would have marched right back to Madame Dufaux asking to see those files again. Of course I wouldn't do that. It was none of my business. But if there was a file on Apolline, wasn't it my duty to make sure the police wouldn't get the wrong idea about her?

My subconscious, or maybe my conscience, made me shiver. No, I couldn't in all honesty make that one stick. Well then, as the daughter of a friend. As the daughter of Apolline's friend, it was my duty to go back and have a look at the files.

I sent a quick text to Madame Dufaux while I kept one ear on the conversation between Apolline and the policemen. They were trying to find out if she knew Louis Lutz, and she only repeated that she had nothing to do with the man, didn't know where her son was, and that he kept his business to himself anyway. Those last words had a definite bitter under-tone, which made me almost feel sorry for Apolline. But then she straightened and put on what she probably considered a friendly smile.

The elder policeman looked up. 'Ah, Monsieur Doo, Brigadier-Chef Dupin.' He held his hand out for Ken to shake. Jacqueline, right next to Ken, went ignored. 'Can you account for your whereabouts around the time of Louis Lutz's death?'

'Yes, he was with me,' Jacqueline's voice answered. I couldn't see her face as she was standing behind Ken, but from the tone of her voice I could imagine the look she gave her colleague.

Though Dupin, as a policeman himself, could probably withstand Jacqueline's withering gaze better than us mere mortals, he did clear his throat and turned back to Apolline.

'If you think of anything else, please call me at this number.' He handed her his card, then had apparently gathered enough courage to address Ken Doo once more. 'We should also like to talk to you and your fellow actors. Can you tell us where they are?'

Ben stepped around me and raised his hand. 'How can I help you, officer?'

Will, never missing an opportunity, also sailed out of the crowd and into the limelight. 'We are at your disposal and ready to cooperate fully,' he announced to the little crowd.

I wondered if he'd go round with a hat after his performance, thinking he must have worked with some pretty good directors if they'd managed to morph all of that attention seeking into a believable performance.

'Is this about the man who died in Saint-Maurice?' Ben asked. 'That has nothing to do with us. I thought he died of natural causes.'

'As a precaution, we'd like to know exactly where you were at the time. Here in France, we take these things seriously. The French police—'

'I was in my room, at the back of the hotel.'

'And I,' Will projected, 'was also in my room. As it overlooks the square and I always like to soak up as much local *ambience* as I can, I had seen the man sitting on that bench, but I'm afraid I didn't see him fall. So, as much as it pains me, I cannot help you.'

'Is that all?' Ben displayed the same attitude he'd had upon arriving at the hotel the day before. I'd grown to like him a bit more, but the fact that he could slip into this arrogance with such ease jarred me.

Both policemen remained impassive, but Dupin said, 'Please provide my colleague with your contact details, in case we need to reach you about this matter. Or anything else.'

Was that a threat or a thinly veiled attempt at getting close to these superstars? I felt like shaking my head, but Apolline did it for me.

As soon as the two had left, she raised her voice to Ben. 'Don't worry. They always like to make you think they have some sort of power over you.' I could make a good guess as to how she knew that. 'Best thing to do is to ignore it. Can I offer you this Euphorbia debilispina?'

My jaw dropped at her audacity. Whether she meant to give him the plant or sell it to him, it was just as blatant an attempt to have her moment in the spotlight as those two policemen had made. All Ben did, however, was shrug and turn away from her to accompany Jacqueline and Ken. I made an effort not to smirk at Apolline's sour face before trying not to show too obviously that I was, in fact, part of the group she was hoping to join.

While Will distracted the crowd by handing out autographs, Ben asked Jacqueline in a low voice, 'Should we be worried?'

Jacqueline shook her head. 'Should be fine. They're just trying to show you their worth. Not every day they meet famous people.'

Ben gave a distracted nod, already losing interest.

I, however, took a step closer to Jacqueline and Ken. 'I thought he died of natural causes. Why are they still investigating?'

She gave me a dark look. 'Those facial injuries were made with malicious intent, but you know I'm not supposed to discuss police matters with you, right?'

I crossed my arms in order to be sassy but was hit by a bout of righteous indignation instead. 'How is this not my business? We still don't know who wrote those words on the hotel window. Who's to say the person who did that to Louis Lutz wasn't also the one painting my window? Is it a coincidence that the two happened so closely together?'

'Yes,' Jacqueline deadpanned. 'I don't see how they could be connected at all.'

She had me there. I'd been thinking about how the two occurrences could have been linked, but I hadn't been able to come up with anything. If Lutz was a blackmailer, he wouldn't write "go home" on a window. He would just use the knowledge for his own gain. Unless someone was blackmailing the blackmailer, but that would just even out the power balance. And whoever had a grudge against Louis Lutz wouldn't have written "go home" on our hotel window, since he lived in the same village. Because the two events happened one after the other, they'd become linked in my head, but if I thought about it logically, there was no way the two were connected.

'And anyway,' Jacqueline continued, 'I'm not on your case any more either. I'm on leave.' And with that, she hooked her arm around Ken's and wandered off, leaving me to the graces of Will, who'd handed out enough autographs and selfies and now came to place his arm around my shoulders. Since he was so much bigger than me, it felt more as if he was using me as an armrest.

'Just you and me now, Juju,' he said, correctly guessing my nickname and pronouncing it correctly, too. 'With your professional experience, I'm sure you can think of lots of ways to have some fun.'

With every word the man uttered, I liked him less. I ducked from underneath his heavy arm, throwing him off balance in the process. 'Is that what you did fifteen years ago? Have some fun?'

His expression turned calculating, and before I could launch into a lecture about how my photographs were empowering, not bawdy, he slinked away. How was a sweetheart like Ken Doo friends with this slime? I made an *ugh* sound to get him out of my system and turned to take some final pictures of Ben when I literally bumped into Beau.

'Where have you been?'

'Saying goodbye to the puppy you wouldn't let me keep,' he moped.

'Not in my house.'

'I know,' he said in a curious way that made me look at him, but he was looking elsewhere. 'I was going to talk to Laurent Tariel, but he seems occupied.'

I followed the line of his vision and spotted the local estate agent in the crowd, laughing and joking with Ben, of all people.

'He didn't strike me as the small talk type,' Beau said.

I considered what I'd seen of Ben. 'He isn't.'

'Well, if your mum is right, Ben must be a drug trafficker too.'

My mother was convinced Monsieur Tariel had ties to the underworld. She seemed to have no other basis for her suspicions than the fact that he was from South America. I'd already told her that she was getting dangerously close to being racist, but she insisted she had reliable sources.

I took a picture, as it was one of Ben with a genuine smile, then decided I'd had enough. I glanced at the big clock on the tower of the chateau. 'It's almost noon. Did you have plans for lunch?'

Thibault shrugged.

'We can't use the hotel, I'm afraid. We're full up with bookings. People trying to catch a glimpse of the film stars,' I explained as we strolled to the car. 'Oh, also, did you want to come along after lunch? I've asked Madame Dufaux if I could have another look at the files in Louis Lutz's house, and she said she'd be there at one.'

'Whose files are we looking at?'

'I, err...' Hm, now that I had to explain why it was imperative that I looked at Apolline's file, it didn't seem so much like my business any more. 'Well, since the police were talking to Apolline...'

Beau snorted. 'You can't keep away from this, can you? Of course I'm coming. Wouldn't miss it for the world.'

12

Poisoned?

We were halfway through our *carrés d'agneau* when my phone interrupted our pleasure. As the screen displayed Madame Dufaux's name, I answered the call, thinking she might be late, which would give us more time to enjoy our food. Unfortunately, her tone conveyed a different message when all she'd said was *bonjour*.

'I've had to call the police,' she blurted.

I frowned, wondering why she'd called me about that. 'I know. Didn't I advise you to do so this morning?'

'No, you don't understand. There's been a break-in.'

My gaze shot to Beau, who lowered his fork in curious anticipation.

'I mean, you can still come over, but all the files, they're in the garden and burnt.'

'We'll be right there.'

As I put the phone away and grabbed my purse, I stood and watched Beau cram in a last few bites of lamb. 'Someone broke in and burnt the files. The police are there now, I think.'

He slowed his chewing and swallowed. 'Then what's the hurry? They're not going to let us in.'

I froze. I was so used to Jacqueline just letting me walk all over her crime scenes that I hadn't considered that her colleagues wouldn't allow me to do so.

'We'll be there for mental support to Madame Dufaux,' I decided, waving my bank card at a waiter.

Twenty minutes later – we ran into a crowd of people wearing hi-vis jackets, engaged in the national pastime of striking and upsetting traffic – I was making a big show of comforting Madame Dufaux. As Thibault had predicted, a policeman had denied us access to the house on the grounds that it was now a crime scene. Instead, they had sent Madame Dufaux out to meet us. She seemed a bit surprised at my emotional display but didn't want to be rude, so she let me carry on.

When the policeman went back inside, I let go of Madame Dufaux and asked her what happened.

'Well, I called the police – like you said – and they said they'd already been – which is true – but that if I thought there was something interesting, then they would be by in due course. But then you asked if you could have another look, and

I thought I'd go in a bit early, because since I'd already inherited everything, I might as well take that diamond painting I showed you home with me. I just wanted a memento. But then when I arrived, there was smoke coming from the garden and when I went back there, a big pile of ashes was smouldering on the lawn. There was nothing I could do. The fire had already died out. I went inside to check, but I was pretty sure it was the files that had been burned. The lock on the back door had been forced, but nothing else had been taken. So then I had to call the police again, and then they finally took me seriously. But of course, then it was too late.' She took a much needed breath.

Yes, too late for me too. Though, with the files gone, the police wouldn't have reason to be talking to Apolline about anything else. 'So do they, or you maybe, have any idea who could have done this?'

Madame Dufaux shrugged. 'There were files on so many people in there, I didn't even know all of them.' Then she frowned. 'Though there was one strange thing. I found a bit of green cardboard at the side of the pile.'

'So whoever took the files also burned the chocolates.' Beau raised his eyebrows so high, his scalp wiggled.

'Did they burn the other sweets too?' I asked.

'No, I checked. Just the *coussins*.'

I pressed my lips together. If whoever burned the files also burned the chocolates, then there must have been something incriminating in them or on them. Had someone tried to bribe their way into Lutz's good graces and left their fingerprint in the process? But if they hadn't burned the chocolates, no one would have given them a second thought. True, they stood out among the cheap chocolates in Lutz's drawer, but even a blackmailer likes to spoil themselves sometimes.

'Did you tell the police what you found?'

'*Oui, c'est normal.* They took a sample, but they said not to make too much of it. Said they were almost sure they were looking for a man, because of the force necessary to break the bones in Monsieur Lutz's face.' She winced when she repeated those words. 'So whoever broke in probably just took one of the chocolates and then realised they had left their fingerprints on the box and burnt it.' She shrugged again, holding up her hands. 'I suppose that's what happened. They're the police, they should know, right?'

I nodded, not wanting to upset Madame Dufaux's trust, but also recalling the pompous way the duo had talked to Apolline. 'Did Monsieur Lutz have any friends?'

When Madame Dufaux started shaking her head, I expanded my question. 'Someone he might consider a colleague? People who came by?'

The shaking continued, so I had to be more direct. 'Did Monsieur Lutz know Constantin Bailly?'

The shaking stopped, and Madame Dufaux tilted her head in thought. 'He knew a lot of people, obviously. It makes more sense now that the people he talked to never really seemed to like talking to him. I've seen him talk to Constantin as well, but...' She put a finger to her lips and then said, 'Actually, you may be right. This was a while ago, last year some time, or maybe even before, that's why I didn't think of it. But I saw Constantin chase Monsieur Lutz down the Rue de Cézanne. Monsieur Lutz clearly didn't want to talk to him as he walked away, but Constantin went after him. It was none of my business, of course, so I kept out of it, but I did think it odd at the time, because most people tried *not* to talk to Monsieur Lutz. Why? Do you think Constantin has anything to do with this?'

Actually, I couldn't think of one good reason why Constantin would be linked with Louis Lutz. I only asked because I'd heard the police asking Apolline about her son. I made a non-committal noise, then offered my help if she needed it with the aftermath, and we said our goodbyes.

Back in the car, Thibault rested his foot against the dashboard, earning him a stern look from me, but he left the appendage where it was.

'So let me get this straight. Lutz was not murdered, so he died of natural causes, but he did roll all the way down a hill that doesn't seem steep enough for him to roll down on his own. Someone mutilated his face after he died. And now it turns out that someone did want to kill him because they sent him poisoned chocolates.'

'Poisoned?' I cried out. 'Where did you get that?'

'Think about it. If all they were worrying about were finger-prints, they would have just taken the box with them and eaten the chocolates. Once they're in your possession, nobody will question your fingerprints on them or whether those choco-lates may have been the ones that were at Louis's house in the first place. But if you knew the chocolates were no good...' He made a hand gesture that finished the thought.

I stared at him.

'Mind the road!' he exclaimed. 'Honestly, I'm surprised you didn't think of this.'

I'd been so preoccupied with the message on the hotel win-dow that I'd failed to see the obvious. Though Louis Lutz had died of natural causes, someone had actually tried to kill him.

I'd stopped at my house but remained in the car. 'We won't know for certain until they analyse the chocolates.' It had to be said, though he and I both knew.

'Formality, trust me.'

For once, I did. 'So, do you have a list of suspects? The police are looking for a man, but who says a woman couldn't be strong enough, if she was angry enough?'

'Isabelle chops meat all day. I'd say she's got some powerful guns there. And you yourself were witness to her anger.'

'Hm. I don't know.' Thinking it over, I exited the car and went into the studio, dangling my purse from my office chair as I picked up my folder of model poses and leafed through it until I found the ones I was going to use that afternoon. 'She was far too eager to admit she'd killed him with her baguette.'

Beau glanced at the picture I held up and opened the props cupboard, from which he pulled a beaten-up box of tools, some dirty coveralls, and a pair of white heels. 'Double bluff? She couldn't have killed him that way so nobody would suspect her of using another method?'

I shook my head. 'If I'm not mistaken, she was covering for someone else. I think she suspected her husband of murdering Louis and she was trying to take the blame.'

Beau frowned, and I told him what I'd seen in the file.

'So, do you think Charles did it?' He said it with a laugh. We both knew Charles was a pussy. Ordinarily, he wouldn't dare do anything without Isabelle's prior approval. But then, he had. And if he'd gone behind his wife's back once...

'There's a big gap between infidelity and murder. Besides, what would be the point? He'd already come clean.' I sighed. 'Judging from the pile of folders in Lutz's cabinet, the list of suspects is endless. I don't think we're going to get very far with this one. And frankly, I'm still more interested in

finding out who painted my window but even there I
haven't got anywhere. I'm pretty sure it was directed at one
of the movie stars, but I don't even know which one. Ken is
the most obvious one since he stayed here the longest in the
past. But he's such a nice guy. I can't imagine anyone having
a grudge against him. But then he did know Lutz and even
went to talk to him because Lutz "knew something". On
the other hand, Will saw him walk away from Lutz. As
much as I don't like the guy and think he should be on the
list, I don't think he lied about that.'

Beau had taken his sketchbook from his back pocket and
was transforming my words into bullet points, to which I
added, 'Tiana told me Monty has some sort of secret, but
she also said it had nothing to do with Saint-Maurice. And
now Ben seems to know our local estate agent. That was
a bit odd, wasn't it? Estate agent, "go home"... Are they
linked?'

Beau tapped his pencil on the notebook. 'I agree that "go
home" was meant for one of them, but you think there's
some sort of link between that and the death of Louis Lutz?'

I took up the box of props and moved to the dressing
room. 'Shouldn't the fact alone that one of them knew him
count for something? Although, that one is Ken.'

'You can't let Jacqueline's romantic feelings get in the
way of logic.'

'But if we count everyone who knew Louis as a suspect, even from the people we know that pool is too large.' I counted on my fingers. 'There's Madame Dufaux. Isabelle, obviously. I'm sure Céline and her dad knew Lutz too, as well as several other people with businesses in Saint-Maurice. I—'

'Of course, it won't be them,' Beau's muffled voice came from between a rainbow of petticoats.

I put my hands on my hips and produced a nasal whine. 'You can't let your romantic feelings get in the way of logic.'

He stuck out his tongue and held up a red petticoat and a baby blue one on either side of his face. I nodded at the red one.

'I recognised several other names of upstanding citizens on the files, including Apolline's.' I sighed again. 'I mean, even Catherine has been acting strangely.'

Beau's eyes flicked between the bright yellow lace-edged granny pants and the pair with white ruffles he held in his hands. 'Really? I hadn't noticed.'

'Were you by any chance holding a puppy in your arms? You know how she loves animals.'

Beau laughed, placing the yellow pants with the red petticoat. 'Yes, I stepped on a snail once, by accident, and she had a right go at me.' He shook his head. 'But she's so boring. What could she possibly have done that's worth blackmailing her for? Ooh, unless—'

I recognised the twinkle in his eye as the precursor to some outlandish and utterly ridiculous theory that wouldn't get us anywhere, so I cut him off. 'Unless you know something I don't, I think we should leave this one to the police.'

He wasn't ready to give up. 'The police are looking for a man because they believe only a man would have the strength to push Louis down the hill. We may not think only a man could do such a thing, but we can exclude people like Madame Dufaux for instance. She simply wouldn't have the strength.'

'True. She could have given him the chocolates, though. But it wouldn't make sense for her to burn them.' Absentmindedly, I picked up a hammer from the toolbox and played with it. 'Do you think the chocolates were sent by the same person who eventually pushed him?'

'You think more than one person might have tried to kill him around the same time? Wouldn't that be a bit of a coincidence? He seems to have been at this blackmail business for a while. Why would two separate people suddenly decide this was it?'

'I don't know. Prices have been going up all over the place; maybe his did too.'

He raised an eyebrow at me. 'I think we can safely say we're dealing with one potential killer.'

I couldn't see why he wouldn't be right so I shrugged. 'And is this person the same one who wrote on my window?'

'Of course not. The person who wanted to kill Louis Lutz was angry with him for blackmailing them, in all probability. The person writing on your window was angry with one of the movie stars, for reasons unknown. The chances that one person would be so angry with both a movie star and a black-mailer at the same time that they'd write on your window and then kill Louis are minuscule.'

I wrinkled my nose. His words, regrettably, made sense. On the one hand I was glad because I didn't have anything to do with the death of Louis Lutz. But I felt silly for being convinced earlier that both instances were linked. 'Good, then I can concentrate on the film stars from now on. Are you coming to the bakery shoot in Villefranche tomorrow?'

'Not unless you need me. But I'm going to see a friend in the city and could use a lift.'

I gave him a thumbs-up as I put down the hammer and went to the door to greet my client. But I couldn't shake the feeling that something Beau had said was wrong.

13

It must have been the hotel owner

The woman coming in for a shoot this afternoon was becoming almost more of a friend than a client. I had counted her among my customers from when I was still selling skin care products online. She'd realised we were both based in Villefranche and could save herself the shipping costs if I agreed to let her pay for coffee every now and then so I could deliver her orders in person. Since this was around the time Franck had cut me off from most of my other friends and family, I'd clutched at the straw she offered me.

Her name was Chantelle Zabu, and she worked in construction. I was always a tiny bit jealous of the muscles rippling under her dark skin. She almost always wore sleeveless tops, so I was convinced she was proud of those muscles too. When I'd asked her to build me a ramp for a client in a wheelchair, she'd refused payment if I would give her a discount on a shoot. I had jumped on that and given her half off, which meant my ramp was the most expensive in existence, but now I had a chance to capture those gorgeous arms on film.

While Maile, my makeup artist, was getting Chantelle ready, she was already chatting away. Happy to see me again, did her ramp do the job, what lovely weather we were having. I could hardly get a word in, but that didn't matter to her. I selected a purple halter dress for her with big, white polka dots. As soon as she saw herself in the mirror, she fell silent. It was not an uncommon reaction, but it still made me smile.

'I look so girly,' she said softly.

I wasn't sure if that was supposed to be a positive or a negative thing until I saw the dampness in her eyes.

She twirled and admired herself from every angle. 'I hardly ever look like a woman any more,' she said. 'This is fantastic. Good to know I still can.'

'And what a woman,' Maile said appreciatively. She'd styled Chantelle's blonde hair into a Marilyn Monroe do, which looked amazing. The only thing I worried about was that my pictures were supposed to look like happy accidents. Chantelle did not look like a woman who would have an accident, happy or otherwise. She was a force to be reckoned with, and I told her as much. At that, she laughed out loud.

'I'm so happy to hear you say that. In my job, I have to look like I'm in total control. If I didn't, those men would walk all over me. Why do you think I talk so much? It's a trick. A coping mechanism. By overshouting my insecurities, I could establish my position. Now, of course, I don't need to do that any more, but it's become a habit.' She twirled again and cooed at herself, 'I'm so pretty.'

I smiled. This appreciation of their own femininity was what gave my clients the happy look that made them buy my photos. But for someone like Chantelle, who had to fight for her femininity, I felt a little extra pride in my work. 'Still, you couldn't pull off a hapless pose where the wind is blowing up your skirt, or it's caught on a fence. How good are you at climbing trees? I know you want to do a Rosie the Riveter, but maybe we can also try Apple of my Eye, or In a Fix. One has you reaching for an apple hanging off a branch, the other makes you pretend to fix the sink.'

'Hey, as long as I get to show off my legs, I'm good.'

'And then some.' Maile grinned. 'After all those men, I think she's happy to focus on a woman again.'

Chantelle's eyes started to sparkle. 'Ooh, that sounds saucy. Who are we talking about?'

'I've been... hm... commissioned to take some touristy photographs of a few male actors who are visiting here from America. They're beautiful people, but men need a different touch from what I'm used to doing. Good thing they wanted candid shots.' I recalled Will's antics from that morning. 'Or already know what pose to take to make them look good.'

'Oh, yes,' Maile acknowledged. 'It's only Will Rice, Ken Doo, Ben Hjerson, and Monty Egg.'

Chantelle's jaw dropped. 'No way. Ben Hjerson? I loved him in *Les Aventures de Monsieur Scott*. He was brilliant. Even after he'd explained how it all happened, I still didn't understand who the villain was.'

At that point, Beau came into the dressing room and he caught the last sentence. 'Are we talking about the dead guy again?'

'What dead guy?' Instead of finding the remark disturbing, Chantelle only got more excited.

This was heading in the wrong direction. 'Let's go to the kitchen,' I proposed. While I opened the cupboard in the fake kitchen that was purely there as a set piece, Beau enlightened Chantelle on the goings-on in our village. He did not neglect to add that he and I had been instrumental in catching some murderers before.

'Ah, so you're Monsieur Scott, are you?'

'Chantelle, lie down here and make sure your face is visible even though I want you to crawl into the cupboard a little bit.' If she got Beau going, I wouldn't get any pictures done today. 'Here's your wrench, so—'

She took the wrench from me and held it up. 'I'm no plumber, but this is completely the wrong tool for the job.'

'You're also not the photographer. Just hold the thing up as if you are fixing the sink.'

'This feels very unfeminist.' Getting down in front of the cupboard, she instead turned back to me. 'I couldn't possibly see what I was doing if I'm supposed to hold my face visible to you.'

Her jab at my feminism had irked me, and I had to suppress a sigh. 'That's irrelevant. You don't need to fix the sink, you just need to be visible and look cute in my picture. Now close one eye as though you've got water into it.'

'Oh, I get it. I'm supposed to wink at the camera, is that it?'

I wiggled my head. 'Kind of. Look surprised. And pull up your skirt so it drapes over your knee. Okay, now, chin forward... and down.' I held up my hand as if guiding her chin forward and down. '*Génial*. Good girl.'

Chantelle was a natural model. I got in some amazing shots right off the bat. But as soon as I told her to get up, it became clear that her mind had not even been on the job.

'So you have four famous film stars staying at your hotel. Someone wants one of the four to go home. And then a notorious blackmailer dies right in front of the hotel. But he wasn't murdered. But his face was bashed in. And someone sent him poisoned chocolates. So obviously, they wanted him dead. So I think...' She paused for dramatic effect. 'It must have been the hotel owner.'

'But *I'm* the hotel owner.'

'No, I mean your partner, the manager.'

I only huffed. Of all the ridiculous theories, this was the most ridiculous. Even if Jeanette hadn't been with me at the time Louis Lutz was mutilated, she simply didn't have it in her. I know that's what people often say about killers, but in her case I was *sur et certain*.

As we made our way into the garden, Chantelle cautioned, 'You can never be too sure of people's innocence.' She herself knew a few people whose face she wouldn't hesitate to bash in if she had the chance, she explained. The more she talked, the more Beau's face twisted, until he looked like he sincerely doubted her sanity.

'Are you sure *you* didn't do it?' Chantelle addressed him. 'You look pretty villainous to me.'

It had taken up till that moment for me to realise that she was messing with him. Thibault, my resident knower of the female mind, still didn't realise.

She puffed up her hair. 'One of my so-called friends insulted my kitty once. I may not have punched his face, but he is no longer my friend.'

I hid a smile at Beau's expression. 'All right, can you get your knee up on this low branch? Make sure your skirt is all the way back and then reach towards that branch as if there was an apple there.'

'But there is no apple.'

'Hence the words "as if". Will fix in post. That's what Photoshop is for.'

She hitched up her skirt and put one foot on the branch. Though the muscles in her leg were beautifully defined, her pose wasn't very elegant.

'No, no, think feminine thoughts. Put your knee on the branch, not your foot.'

She replaced her foot with her knee but still didn't look very appealing.

'Pointy toes, please. You're wearing heels for a reason.'

'And that's why I never wear heels ordinarily. Who wants to be on their toes all day?'

I kept diplomatically quiet on that one. Since I was vertically challenged, I needed the extra height even when doing a shoot. The only time I did not wear heels was when I was on a hike with Jacqueline. 'It's just for the picture. Make me some Barbie feet.'

Chantelle rolled her eyes but stretched her body into the perfect pin-up pose and I eagerly clicked away.

'Excellent,' Beau commented. 'You could easily join the superheroes.'

Chantelle pointed at her Marilyn waves. 'Got the blonde hair and everything.' She twisted round so she could sit on the branch, her feet dangling just above the ground, and twisted a lock around her finger. 'Do you think it suits me? I'm still not sure. I'm what they call mixed race, but it's a stupid term. Aren't we all the human race?' She hopped off the branch, but her skirt caught on a knot, and I snapped the perfect natural accidental picture. This might just be the best shoot I'd ever done.

'Well, except for the superheroes of course,' Beau said.

'Maybe that's why I don't care for superheroes. I like those guys though. There was one episode of *Monsieur Scott* where they thought it was the victim's colleague who'd done it, but then they found evidence of blackmail and they thought it was the colleague's lover who'd done it, but in the end it turned out to be a monkey.' She made a face.

'You know, that actually happened,' Beau mused. 'One of the earliest forensic scientists was based here in Lyon. His name was Edmond Locard and he fingerprinted monkeys after a series of mysterious thefts. Sometimes the victims were left without valuable jewellery, but other times things were stolen that didn't seem to have any intrinsic value. The only thing that connected all of these thefts was that the thief had entered through a very high window. Locard was correct. An organ grinder's monkey was found to be the thief. The organ grinder went to jail, and the monkey went to the local zoo.'

Both Chantelle and I stared at Beau. 'You know the strangest things,' I said.

'My dad told us to always know your enemies.'

Not for the first time I was glad my family stayed on the right side of the law. That cleaning products factory Beau's dad owned was the only above-board enterprise in the whole family. Though I suspected it was little more than a front for more nefarious activities. Officially, they all worked there, but some, I was sure, had never even been inside the building.

Chantelle shrugged. 'Maybe that's where they got the idea. But it seemed a pretty convoluted plot to me. Like your man in the village. If you're gonna smash someone's face in, it's far more likely to have happened in a jealous rage than after careful plotting.'

'Not if the person's already dead.' My camera hung forgotten in my hip holster. Chantelle seemed more interested in solving the mystery than in having her picture taken, but I had enough for a beautiful spread.

'No, that seems more of a vindictive action. The person who beat him must have felt seriously wronged. Which is kind of strange considering the victim was a blackmailer. Whoever hit him must have done something wrong in the first place to be blackmailed about it. They must have hated him for pointing out their shortcomings, which sounds rather narcissistic to me.'

'Enough to send him poisoned *coussins* chocolates too?'

'I don't know. I'll tell you what, though. No woman would poison those things unless they were crazy rich. Now, how about I flex my muscles and do my Rosie the Riveter?'

14

A giant croissant

Jacqueline had not felt happier in years. Ken was still the same man she knew fifteen years ago, so Hollywood hadn't changed him. Of course, he'd matured somewhat; so had she. But where she'd become jaded and cynical, he still saw the world with eyes full of wonder, grateful for every blade of grass on his path. Talking to him after all these years was like stepping from a pigsty into a tea shop.

The pigsty had been her life. Whenever she'd had to take time off, she was only waiting to get started again. But with Ken, everything was different. She had no desire to get back to the pigsty. What that meant for the moment he'd return to America, she did not want to think about. For once, she was going to enjoy whatever life threw at her right now.

After a delightful day of being together, talking, getting to know each other again, kissing... and an evening of catching up even more, she decided not to go back to her apartment, but ask an aunt who lived in Saint-Maurice if she could stay for the night. Now, she was leaning out the first-story window, breathing in the cool country air. She'd only gone to the window to close the shutters, but the vast array of stars had distracted her. The light pollution in Villefranche meant she could never see this many stars from her apartment. While she loved living in the busyness of the city, the countryside did have its merits.

Her aunt's house was on the main street of Saint-Maurice, just around the corner from the hotel. But the busiest this street ever got was around the start and end times of the village school. This time of night, there was no—

'This is ridiculous!' she suddenly heard someone whisper outside. In the stillness, even a whisper was clearly audible from above. Jacqueline tried to lean out unobtrusively but couldn't see who was talking.

'I told you you shouldn't be here!' the whispering person continued.

'Yes. Subtle, that.'

Though the voice was low, Jacqueline recognised it immediately. It was Will Rice. If this person didn't want Will here, and they'd left an unsubtle message, was this the person who'd written "go home" on the hotel window? Jacqueline tried to get another look but though she could see Will's back, the other person was hidden behind him.

'Why can't you just leave me alone?'

'You're delusional!' Will lowered his voice back to a whisper. 'I didn't come here for you.'

'No? Then why did I get a reminder now, after so long?'

Will didn't immediately answer. 'I don't know, maybe he found out.'

'He didn't contact you?'

'I thought it was all in the past. Not that it's not nice to see you.'

'You're a creep and you always have been.'

The corner of Jacqueline's mouth lifted. Whoever this person was, they had a good grasp of Will's character.

'Hey, I get a lot of money for doing what you used to do,' Will retorted. 'Pretend you're something you're not.'

There was a short silence, and then the whispered voice came again. 'Stay. Away. From me.'

'No problem, *ma puce*.'

The street stayed quiet after that.

The whole conversation had been odd, but the last bit was particularly confusing. *Ma puce*, my little flea, was usually something said to little girls. But though the voice did sound like it was a woman's, she most certainly was not a little girl. It was likely that this woman had painted the hotel window. And if the message had been meant for Will, Jacqueline wholeheartedly agreed with the sentiment, if not with the action.

Even if she had to fine the mystery woman later, they had at least one thing in common: a thorough dislike of Will Rice.

The next morning, Jacqueline was at the hotel bright and early. Ken probably wouldn't have much time for her today, as it was the day of his baking course, but she wanted to be there for him nonetheless. Before that, however, Jacqueline needed to talk to Will. She might not be on the case, or even on duty right now, but she needed to convince him to tell either her or her colleagues what he knew. Julie was still worried about why someone would paint on her window, and the police needed to know if this occurrence had anything to do with the death of Louis Lutz. Will's knowledge could mean peace of mind for the one, and a breakthrough in the case for the other. If anything, Jacqueline did not want Will Rice to hold such power.

He wasn't likely to give up this information easily, though. For one, it was connected to some kind of wrongdoing in his past involving this woman. Why else keep it secret? Secondly, he hadn't said anything to disclose the identity of the woman before, so perhaps he was trying to protect her? Jacqueline shook her head. Ken's optimism was getting to her. If Will said anything about the woman, he would implicate himself. He was only protecting his own hide.

Still, she felt she had to try to get through to him. She'd sent him a text early this morning telling him to meet her here in the hotel lounge ten minutes ago. That he was late didn't surprise her. She only hoped he'd seen the text at all. Will had never been one for mornings, preferring to forego breakfast and go straight to lunch from his bed. She had made herself comfortable and was scanning the latest on the gang wars in one of the hotel newspapers, not expecting Will to show up any time soon, when he threw himself on the chair opposite her like a sack of potatoes.

'This had better be important. If you're going to nag me about Ken's career, I'm going back to bed.' Despite it being July and already a warm morning, he wore a chunky jumper and hunched a little, trying to hide the fact that he had too much muscle to be an ordinary bloke.

Jacqueline narrowed her eyes at him. 'Who wrote the message on the window? I know it was meant for you.'

Will's jaw went slack as her stared at her. 'How'd...' But then he checked his surprise and sat up straight. 'I won't tell you.'

Jacqueline said nothing but kept her eyes on him. Eventually, almost everyone said more, and Will was no exception.

'The paint's cleaned up. There's no harm done. You don't need to know.'

'A man is dead.'

Will waved his hand through the air. 'That has nothing to do with h— with this. You said yourself he died of natural causes.'

'Someone still ruined his face. That's a violent act.'

'And there is nothing violent about writing on a window. S—Someone... is not the same person.'

'Oh, you're here already.' Contrary to Will, Ken had always been a morning person. He made a beeline for Jacqueline, but his look turned puzzled when he spotted Will.

'Couldn't sleep.' Will stretched and yawned convincingly; he'd made his expression carefully neutral the moment he heard Ken's greeting. 'Must still be jet-lagged or something. Thought I'd entertain your girl in your absence, but she doesn't seem to want me. Must be the colour of my hair.'

Ken's smile stretched even more widely. 'I thought you would have learned your lesson by now. My girls are too smart to fall for your lines.'

It was an innocent joke, but Jacqueline still felt a little stab of jealousy at the mention of Ken's girls. Of course he'd had girlfriends in all those years. She herself had been attracted to other men in the meantime, but none of them had measured up to Ken. And isn't that what Ken himself had said? No one compared to her?

Ken turned to Jacqueline and kissed her. 'Good morning, *chérie*. I hope you slept well.'

'Exceedingly. Ready to bake some pastries?'

'You bet. I dreamt I was making this giant croissant with—'

A loud, fake snore came from Will. 'I'm gonna go back to bed. I don't even care if I dream about croissants or not. Sorry, mate, but I think I'll skip the party today.'

Jacqueline gave a tight smile as Will rose and left. He was lucky to have a friend as guileless as Ken. If she had her say... But then, what was she? Ken had done without her for so long, and though they'd had the same immediate connection, making them fall for each other all over again, they hadn't spoken about what would happen when Ken returned to the US.

Fifteen years ago, she didn't want to be in his way, and she'd had her own career to think about. But now, were things different? His career was well-established, and hers... It was all she knew. She'd never even considered doing anything else. Would she now, if he asked her to?

But why would he? He was only here for a few days. Even if she was special to him, did they really know each other any more?

'You still don't like him, do you?' Ken's question took her out of her contemplations.

'He hasn't changed that much.'

'Neither have I, I hope.'

Jacqueline huffed a laugh. 'No, you seem just the same.'

'Better for having you around.'

She smiled, but didn't dare voice the thoughts she'd just had.
'So, a giant croissant, eh?'

Ken was happily whacking dough with a rolling pin and joking
about it being a true superhero workout. The group of people
following the pastry chef's orders was small – Ken, Ben, Monty, and two middle-aged women who couldn't believe their
luck. Julie flitted around taking pictures. Jacqueline was there
only to be close to Ken, since she had no inclination to bake
anything ever, so she kept mostly to the edges of the stainless
steel room, wondering how nobody had been murdered in
here yet with all those weapons around.

Yet again, she reminded herself that normal people look
around a kitchen and think of food, rather than death
when Dupin and Rouletabille surreptitiously entered the
kitchen. She wondered what her colleagues' first thoughts
were. Jacqueline knew they were only doing their job, but now
that it was aimed at someone she cared for, she couldn't help
going up to them and asking, 'Couldn't this have waited?'

Dupin puffed up his chest. 'I know you're usually a good
cop, so I'll do you a favour and overlook your obvious partiality

in this, but *entre nous*, the chocolates were poisoned. And look who just happens to have an interest in food.'

He gestured at Ken Doo with a look that managed to be both pompous and pitying.

'You're not seriously accusing a Hollywood superstar of poisoning chocolates to send to some obscure French black-mailer.'

Of course, Ken's stardom had nothing to do with whether or not he could be a suspect in an investigation, but Jacque-line had already experienced her colleagues' sensitivities in that area, and her words hit their mark.

Dupin held up both hands in defence and shook his head. 'No, no, of course not. I mean, it's poison. We're probably looking for a woman. And there was no trace of it in the victim's body, so she's probably going to get off lightly. But I still maintain that the wounds to the face were caused by a man.'

'So Ken is a suspect because he likes to cook, but not because the chocolates were poisoned, but because you think a man hit Louis Lutz in the face.'

She could see the wheels turning inside Dupin's thick skull, but he wasn't about to let a woman throw him off course.

'We have to follow every possible lead, you know that.'

That, she couldn't argue with. 'So which lead are you fol-lowing in this?'

'The fact that your *friend*' – he emphasised the word as if it were something dirty – 'knew the victim.'

Jacqueline nodded once. She'd been meaning to ask Ken about his connection to Lutz. Now she'd have to let Dupin bumble his way through that line of questioning. The uncomfortable realisation dawned on her that having Ken here again had closed her eyes to unpleasant possibilities. But then, there was no way Ken was involved with Louis Lutz. Neither as a friend nor as a policewoman could she be convinced of that.

While Dupin and Rouletabille went to bother Ken, Julie shuffled up to Jacqueline, her camera bouncing in its hip holster. 'Why are they still after him?'

'He knew Lutz.' Jacqueline watched her colleagues take Ken to a little office area off to the side. She'd been hoping to listen in, but this way she couldn't come to Ken's aid. Not that he needed it, of course.

Julie was also eyeing the office, worrying her bottom lip and obviously not asking a question.

'What is it?' Jacqueline asked to speed along the process.

'Oh, nothing.'

'Out with it.'

'Were the chocolates poisoned?' She twisted her face as if expecting a torrent of rage.

But Jacqueline knew her friend long enough by now to expect the unexpected. 'Do I even want to know how you know?'

'Actually, Beau figured that out,' she said, beaming like a proud mother.

'Don't tell me. You have a theory.' As much as she tried to discourage Julie's involvement in police matters, especially as she had been instrumental in getting her into them in the first place, Jacqueline was impressed with how often Julie's theories turned out to be at least close to the truth.

'Well, I don't know if you noticed, but those stars aren't as shiny as they make out to be.'

'Are you including Ken in that assessment?'

Julie flicked her dark brown ponytail. 'I mean, has he told you how he knew Lutz?'

Straight to the point. A quality Jacqueline usually preferred to beating around the bush, but in this case, the point hurt. 'I hadn't asked.'

'Their connection is probably innocent enough. But Ben tried to distract me when I was talking to him about plants. And Tiana is adamant that Monty has some sort of secret. And Will—'

'I know about Will,' Jacqueline interrupted.

Julie turned from staring at the office to face Jacqueline, hoping for more, but she should know by now that Jacqueline was not the gossiping type. Besides, though she knew Will knew who had defaced the hotel window, she didn't know why this person wanted Will gone. From what she'd heard, the woman had got a reminder of past indiscretions. The most likely candidate to have reminded her would be Louis Lutz, but Will had assured her the two weren't connected.

She asked Julie, 'So what is your theory?'

The corners of Julie's mouth turned down with a stubborn pique. 'You tell me. I was going to say Will is the most likely suspect, but you say you already know about Will. If you don't need my theory, why ask for it?'

'Why do you suspect Will?' Jacqueline didn't need to offer her friend anything. Julie would tell her all about it anyway, as she was always far too excited about what she'd deduced to keep quiet.

'I don't know if I'm influenced by this Louis Lutz business, but I keep thinking Will must have something on Ken if he's tolerated him for so long. Why else would Ken hang around with such a creep?'

'Can't arrest a man for being a creep. Our cells would always be overflowing.'

'I've only been thinking about who could have written the message on my window. Literally anyone could have killed Louis Lutz because he made enemies all over the place. Except of course for anyone without the physical strength to administer those injuries. But that still leaves us with too many unknown suspects. "Go home", however, seems most likely meant for one of the film stars. Ben has only ever been to Paris before now, and Monty has been to the Cannes film festival but never to this area. That leaves Ken and Will. Call me crazy, but out of those two I know who my suspect would be.'

An interesting theory, and one Jacqueline could get behind, but there wasn't much real evidence for it. Perhaps Julie's brain would work out more of the mystery if she had more information, after all. 'Since it's your window, I suppose you should know that you are correct. The message was meant for Will. He knows who wrote it, but he won't tell me who it was. Says he is certain they had nothing to do with Louis Lutz's death.'

'So the police should be talking to him instead.'

'Yes, they should. As soon as they are done talking to Ken, I will make sure they do.'

'But Will must know that they are coming for him. He'll have his story ready.'

'So maybe we can find out ourselves?' Jacqueline looked her friend in the eye. 'You live in Saint-Maurice. You might know who from the village was around in Villefranche fifteen years ago, when Will was in the city. I think we can safely say the paint on the window was a moment of opportunity for a local, not someone who came from Villefranche on the off-chance they'd find the square and the hotel lobby empty. Will was only here for about a month, but I can give you the exact dates. I heard him talking to a woman last night – at least, I'm pretty sure it was a woman. I'm sure their conversation had something to do with his time here. He called her *ma puce*, which means she probably would have been quite a young girl at the time. But either Will is a lot creepier than I would give him credit for...'

Julie recoiled, and Jacqueline gave a slight shake of her head. 'No, she would have used a different tone with him if that were the case, even if she did call him a creep. But I just can't figure out what the two of them could have been up to that would make her write "go home" on a hotel window fifteen years later.'

'Fifteen years ago I was a teenager. If he called her *ma puce*, she's probably my age or younger but no younger than about twenty, I would say, if she was really very young then. I can give you a list of girls who lived in Villefranche at the time and in the village now – I'll ask my friends to look at it too. It'll probably still be quite a big list, though.'

At that moment, Ken reappeared from the office. Even after being harassed by Dupin and Rouletabille, the gorgeous man was still smiling, but there was a pensive aspect to his gaze. He took his place at the worktop and the police officers disappeared with a nod to Jacqueline.

She was dying to talk to Ken but he was hurrying to catch up with the others. Julie went back to taking pictures, but in her place, Monty Egg joined Jacqueline.

'Do you think it's serious? They're not going to pin anything on him, are they?'

'No, they're just trying to be thorough,' she said, reassuring him as much as herself. 'Haven't they talked to you yet?'

'Sure, but I couldn't tell them anything. My room's at the back of the hotel, and I've never been here before. I had no idea who the man was, or that Ken knew him. As far as holidays go, this has turned into a memorable one. But why question Ken again? They'd already interviewed all of us.'

'The victim was sent a box of poisoned chocolates. And Ken likes food.'

Jacqueline had expected Monty to comment on the thinness of the connection, but instead, he blanched.

'Chocolates? Not those green boxes of boozy chocolates?'

Jacqueline frowned. 'Yes, why?'

'No reason. It's a crime to poison those things. They're delicious.'

'You need to tell me what you know.' Jacqueline had wanted to keep the hardness out of her voice as she was talking to one of Ken's friends, but because of her concern for him, she'd slipped into professional mode. The upside of that was that Monty immediately obliged.

His eyes darted left and right before he said anything and then cast his gaze down to his fidgeting fingers before he admitted, 'Will asked me to buy him a box of those chocolates in Lyon, before we came here. I hadn't seen him eat them, though, so I assumed he'd sent them to a friend. I still think he did that,' he added quickly.

'Hm. I'm sure he did.'

Only partly comforted, Monty returned to his own workspace. The workshop didn't last much longer after that, and the participants moved towards the little café attached to the bakery. In contrast to the sterile stainless steel surfaces of the kitchen, the café contained an explosion of trinkets and ornaments on pristine doilies and tablecloths with lace edges. Jacqueline preferred the clean lines of the kitchen, but as soon as she took a bite of her white chocolate and blueberry macaron, she forgave the owners their taste in decoration.

She shared a table with Julie, Ken, Monty, and Ben, sipping coffee and eating their own fresh pastries. Eyeing Monty's chocolate croissant, Jacqueline was quite happy to have been able to choose from a real cook's assortment, though Ken's *pain au raisins* looked perfect. Everyone was quiet apart from some expressions of appreciation until Ben put down his *chausson au pomme* and said to Ken, 'This is a load of tosh. We should be enjoying our top-notch sweet treat instead of wondering if we'll have to answer for our actions again. Just tell us if we should make a complaint about the behaviour of those policemen.'

Ken straightened. 'No, of course not. All they did was ask me if I knew about computers. I asked them what they meant, and they said Lutz's hard drive had been stolen. Look, you all might as well know how I knew Louis Lutz. When I was here fifteen years ago, that time I met Jacqueline, Will was with me as well. Will... got into some trouble.' A few eye-rolls made him change that statement. 'Actually, it was a friend of his who got into trouble. With Lutz. Will only wanted to help, but he couldn't be attached to a scandal because he didn't want to implicate his family, because of, you know, their social standing. He asked me to go to Lutz in his stead, to pay the man a ransom.'

Ben huffed and muttered, 'Social standing.'

Jacqueline took her eyes off Ken for a half-second glance at the Brit. His attitude spoke volumes, but as Ken continued, Jacqueline had to let go of her curiosity on that front.

'As far as I knew, the whole thing was done and dusted after I did that. But when we were set to come here again, I received a note from Louis Lutz. He knew I was the same person who'd approached him back then, and he thought that because I was now famous, he could apply new pressure. That's why I went to see him that morning. I told him he could take his pressure and stick it. He laughed and said, "We'll see about that." But I turned and walked away and never saw him again. I know how it looks, and that's why I'm not surprised the police wanted to talk to me again, but I've been in plain sight ever since, and so I couldn't have been the one burning the files or stealing the hard drive from Lutz's home.'

'And you didn't buy any chocolates,' Monty added.

'Err, no?'

Monty explained about the poisoned chocolates and the box of them that he'd bought in Lyon for Will.

'You can't possibly suspect Will of trying to poison Louis Lutz,' Ken said. That closed the subject for him, but the others didn't seem so sure. Ben and Monty exchanged a look. It seemed Jacqueline was not the only one with a dislike for Will Rice. As much as she loved Ken's optimism and loyalty, she was glad to see the other two were a bit more sceptical about Will's innocence.

Focusing back on Ken, though, she had to remind herself that she couldn't accuse a man of a crime simply because she didn't like him or thought his behaviour towards his friends was unfair or even exploitative. Ben's reaction just now made her suspect Ken was not the only one of Will's friends who'd had to deal with his selfishness.

But selfishness was not a crime. Going forward, she'd have to be careful not to twist any new evidence to fit her own purpose: protecting the beauty that was Ken's soul. A beauty she was getting more and more convinced she would not be able to let go of any more.

15

Stop looking

The July sun stung my eyes as we exited the café onto the busy streets of Villefranche, so I donned my sunglasses. But what I could then see almost made me take them off again. Across the street from the café, Anne-Bonny was prancing around in another one of her ridiculous outfits. She'd found out where we were *again*. This time, I was sure nobody knew where we would be going, so seeing her was a surprise, and a very unwelcome one at that. How had she found out where we'd be? Could she truly have Franck's hacking skills? Or was she working with him? But why follow me around when she lived right next to me? Was this Franck's way of letting me know he was keeping an eye on me?

Trying not to be too obvious, I glanced her way once more while pretending to check my phone. She was talking to none other than Isabelle Cochon, who was leaning on a bright red sports car that she'd only had for a week. Now that I knew of her husband's indiscretion, I had a suspicion as to why she was suddenly driving around in a brand new car. But what was

Isabelle doing in Villefranche? And talking to Anne-Bonny no less. She'd been trying to catch everyone's attention, saying she murdered Louis Lutz. But though she obviously hadn't done that, she was the only one I knew who had recently been a victim of his blackmail schemes.

What I hadn't told Jacqueline was that I'd had a bit of a disturbing message in my inbox this morning. It came from a sender named Not A. Killer, and all it said was *Stop looking*. If that was supposed to scare me, it didn't work. I wasn't looking! Well, I was, but I was only trying to find out who wrote on my window. And now Jacqueline had told me Will knew who it was, I wouldn't have to look anywhere but at the list of women who lived in Saint-Maurice now but could have been in Villefranche fifteen years ago. Though it was obvious why they wouldn't want me to find out who they were, sending me anonymous messages only made me more curious.

Beau had not shared that sentiment. For one, he didn't believe the message came from the window writer. He said it came from the poisoned-chocolates sender, and I should be aware of what I ate from now on.

But the message had come from *Not* A. Killer. Didn't that say enough? He was not convinced and told me to be careful. But all his concern had done was make me curious as to who had sent the chocolates. If Beau was right about that, and it was the potential killer who was warning me – even though they called themselves *not* a killer – they must know a bit about what was going on in the village, and therefore it must have been a local. A local who had had dealings with Louis Lutz. Like Isabelle.

Anne-Bonny spotted the movie stars and came over to say hi, as if she was their oldest friend. That's when I decided there was no time like the present and I crossed the road to speak to Isabelle.

'Nice car. New?' I asked.

'It's my pride and joy. I've been nagging Charles for so long, and suddenly he was okay with me getting one. So here it is. What do you think?'

'I think it suits you,' I said truthfully. The flashy red was just her thing, and the car's speed would no doubt help her jump to conclusions even more quickly. 'To be honest, Isabelle, I've been to Lutz's house. I've seen your file. Don't worry,' I added when I saw her pale, 'I won't tell anyone. But in order to find out who might have had a grudge against him, I'd like you to tell me what happened in your case. Did he come to you personally? Or leave a note, or something?'

Isabelle took a few deep breaths, glaring at me like a bull about to charge. I expected her to dismiss me with a few choice words, but instead, her breathing calmed, and her shoulders sagged.

'Actually, I'm glad someone knows. I'm sure everyone else will find out soon enough. But I know you at least can be trusted.'

I was strangely touched by her words. Much as Isabelle liked to gossip, she did usually have quite a good insight into people's characters. So the fact that she would trust me made me glow a little on the inside.

'Lutz made the mistake of sending a letter to our house, instead of to Charles. Once I'd opened it, all Charles could do was confess. I was devastated. I left to live with my mother for a while, but before I left, I made sure Louis Lutz would know not to expect anything from us.'

'So you believed him?'

'He'd included a photograph. Said not to make the mistake of thinking that was the original. I don't even care any more if someone does find the original. Charles has assured me it was a one-time thing, and I intend to believe him.'

I gave Isabelle a sympathetic smile and said I applauded her. I also let her know that the files had been destroyed so she wouldn't have to worry about the picture getting into the wrong hands. Then I crossed the street to rejoin Ken and Jacqueline, who were standing a few feet away from Ben and Monty, who had been roped into taking selfies with Anne-Bonny again.

'Where did she come from?' Jacqueline asked, inclining her head at the ever-present influencer.

'I wish I knew,' I sighed. But instead of dwelling on the unpleasant implications of Anne-Bonny's presence, I just had to gloat to Jacqueline about what she'd told me earlier. 'So there was in fact a connection between the window and Lutz.'

Jacqueline smiled. 'All right, I'll give you that one.' She turned to Ken. 'The message on the window was meant for Will. He told me as much. But he won't tell me who did it. Are you sure you don't remember the name of the girl he was protecting all those years ago?'

'Or perhaps her age?' I added.

'It was a long time ago,' Ken answered in unusually flat tones.

But he didn't dispute that the matter involved a girl.

'I've had to tell Dupin and Rouletabille to ask him about it,' Jacqueline continued. 'If he won't tell them what he knows, that's perverting the course of justice, and he could go to jail. You need to talk to him.'

Ken only gave a short nod, and I could feel the distance between him and Jacqueline growing. If I didn't like Will before, I certainly couldn't stand him now. He was getting in the way of my friend's happiness. Now, I'm not one to butt in where I'm not wanted, but if I had a chance to talk to Will, I certainly would.

For now though, Isabelle's words had got me thinking. Not all evidence of indiscretions had to be on paper. Could there still be evidence in Louis Lutz's house of other people faults? I remembered the out-of-place clay ashtray and the solitary book, and even the painting Louis himself had labelled 'a picture of a murderer'.

I left the others with the excuse of having to work on my photo editing, but as soon as I was out of earshot, I called Madame Dufaux. 'I'm sorry to bother you again, but would you mind letting me into Louis Lutz's house one more time?'

She agreed to meet me there, and when I arrived, she got out of her own car and unlocked the door. 'Where's your shadow?'

I pressed my lips together. My so-called assistant had let me know 'he had something to do' in Villefranche. I'd agreed to drop him off and he said he'd make his own way back. I'd told him that was short notice and I'd consider it annual leave, but he'd only laughed and shrugged. I hoped I would find a massive clue in Lutz's house while he had apparently more pressing matters to attend to.

'Getting supplies,' I lied to Madame Dufaux.

'I don't know what you expect to find,' she said, leading me into the house. 'The police have been over the place with a fine-tooth comb after the files were burned.'

'Maybe they didn't know what they were looking for.'

'Do you?'

'Not really, but perhaps something will stand out.' As soon as I entered the living room, I went straight for the ashtray on the coffee table. Turning it around, I saw some writing on the bottom. *À Papa Philippe*, it said in childish letters. 'Do you know any Philippes?' I asked Madame Dufaux.

'Several, why?'

'Any that are not supposed to be dads?'

She shook her head, and I replaced the ashtray. I didn't know why exactly, but I'd had high hopes for that ashtray. I couldn't think how it could possibly be linked to my case, but it was such a strange object in this room that it screamed *clue* at me. Of course, in a way, it was. I was very probably right about it being some sort of evidence against someone's secret, but it had nothing to do with me or the people I wanted to find out about.

I turned to the one book on the filing cabinet, much less confident than I'd been before. Again, I was right. Stuck to the title page was a note, thanking Daniel for getting a student into a prestigious program. The person hoped the book would be accepted as a sincere expression of gratitude in addition to 'agreed terms'. The note in the book explained why I'd seen Lutz coming from Catherine and Daniel's house, but it didn't help me on my current quest. I closed the book with a thump.

Now what? I looked around for any other objects that looked out of place. But these two had only looked out of place because there wasn't anything else.

'Is there anything upstairs that doesn't seem like it should be there?'

'I don't know. I always thought these things belonged here too.'

My gaze passed over all the empty surfaces and angular furniture. 'Did the police look in the cupboards?'

'They did, but they wouldn't have found anything interesting. Even the broom cupboard just holds the broom.'

I'd wandered over to the computer by the window. Other than the missing system unit that the police had taken away, the desk looked just as stark as the rest of the house. I leaned on the window sill, hoping my overview of the room from this point by the desk would give me some new insight. But it was only when I looked closer that I found a framed photograph hidden behind the curtain. It showed a pretty, young Latina woman.

'Do you recognise her?' I asked Madame Dufaux.

She came near and took the photograph from me, studying the woman in the picture. 'Can't say that I do. Monsieur Lutz never mentioned her.'

'Do you mind if I take it out of the frame? Perhaps there's something written on the back.'

'Go ahead. I don't think Monsieur Lutz is going to mind.'

It was a long shot, but my efforts paid off. On the back of the picture were two words: Madame Tariel.

Madame Dufaux looked at me with raised eyebrows. 'I didn't know Monsieur Tariel was married.'

Neither did I. A pretty woman like that would have been noticed in Saint-Maurice, but the estate agent had never been romantically linked to any woman, as far as I knew. Though this was certainly another of Louis Lutz's pieces of evidence for his blackmailing operation, it wasn't going to help me identify the woman who was telling Will Rice to go home. Another dead end.

'Do you think there's something on the back of the painting?' Madame Dufaux pointed at the lady with the plant hanging above the TV.

I blinked. I hadn't even thought of that. I rushed over to the painting and took it off its hook. But when I flipped it over, there was nothing on the back, not even a label. I flipped it back to see if there was a signature, but there didn't seem to be any. Carefully, I hung the painting back.

'Well, that was disappointing.' Madame Dufaux crossed her arms. 'I really thought you had something there. Now, we may never find out who was after Monsieur Lutz's life.'

I pressed my lips together in frustration. I'd thought I had something too. But though I'd found some evidence implicating someone named Philippe, Tiana's neighbour Daniel, and possibly Monsieur Tariel, none of them seemed to be a plausible murderer. And they were all men, so they didn't qualify for my window besmircher. 'We'll have to hope the police find something on his computer.'

'But the burglar took the hard drive.'

'I know.' Louis's death may have had nothing to do with me, but I couldn't help feeling responsible in some way. It was now obvious that the person who'd written on my window also had something to do with Louis Lutz, but according to Will Rice, they were not the killer.

My gaze rested on the ashtray, the painting, the book, and the photograph in turn, and I frowned. The whole thing was frustratingly out of focus. If I was ever going to get a clear picture, I needed a new lens.

16

I know, you know

Will Rice was going to talk. If not to the police, then to me. Why he would deign to do so I didn't yet know, but I would think of something. I went up to Monty's room, where we had agreed to meet before travelling together to the Festival de Livre. It was held in the Marché Couvert in Villefranche, a place famous for never having enough parking space. If we could squeeze ourselves into one car, there'd be a better chance of us finding a space. Apparently, the people in Villefranche wouldn't give up their parking spaces, even for a famous movie star or three.

When I entered the room, the others were in spirited conversation. The police were interviewing Will right now. So much for my plan – he was talking to them, not to me.

'I don't care!' Ben was saying, in answer to someone else's suggestion. 'They've been coming after us like hounds on a trail. I'm not in the mood to be vilified by some Frenchies.'

'I have to say,' Monty agreed, 'we've done nothing wrong. Why do they keep harassing us?' He looked at Jacqueline, but it was Ken who answered.

'In my case, it's obvious. I did talk to the man.'

'Yes, but it was about Will.' Ben balled up a piece of paper he'd been holding and threw it in the bin. 'It's always about Will, isn't it?'

They were silent after Ben's outburst, and I moved from the door I'd quietly closed behind me to the little desk at the window where Jacqueline was sitting. She didn't seem too bothered with the attack on her... erm... 'friend's' friend. In fact, unless I was very much mistaken, I saw a hint of amusement in her otherwise impassive face.

Ken took a deep, long-suffering breath. 'He's not—'

'Really like that, yes, we know. You've only said it a hundred times before. It might be nice if he showed his real self every now and then, though.' Clearly Ben was not happy with Will joining their trip. Or even their group of friends.

After a pause, Monty changed the subject. 'I'm sorry to be a nuisance, but if we're going to go, we should go now.'

The other men stood up immediately.

'Right you are,' Ben said at the same time as Ken's 'Of course.'

'He can always join us later, and if not, we can catch up afterwards,' Monty added, but the others were already on their way out of the room.

Jacqueline and I followed the men at a slight distance.

'What did I miss?' I asked her.

'They don't like Will,' Jacqueline said, her satisfaction obvious now. 'Those two don't like the fact that Will could tell the police something that could possibly clear Ken but that he is not talking. Apparently, my esteemed colleagues talked to Ben again as well, which he did not care for. Monty is the only one who's had no more than a casual conversation with them.'

'Huh,' I mused. 'Perhaps my mother is right after all. Do you know a Laurent Tariel?'

'No, should I?'

'My mother thinks he has drug connections. And Beau and I saw him talking to Ben this morning.'

'Drugs? Ben? Are you serious? I think the only reason they talked to Ben again was that he is married to a French woman.'

'That makes more sense.' I nodded, both of us dismissing my mother's drugs theory.

I deposited my camera bag in the trunk of the waiting limousine. A limousine! No parking space necessary. So this was how the other half lived. On the way over, we only discussed books. I made sure to mention my friend Tiana, who wrote romance novels, but Ken only read fantasy, and Ben was not much of a reader. Said he liked thrillers when he did pick up a book. Monty, however, was enthusiastic. He told me he always carried a book with him wherever he went, and he read a bit of everything. That's why he was so excited about this festival. He was hoping to find some new French authors he didn't know about.

'Do you read French?' I asked him.

'My mother was French. She taught me to read it, but I don't speak it very well.'

Jacqueline took over at this point, trying to get him to speak French with her for a bit. But my thoughts ran away with me. Somehow, everyone in this company seemed to have some sort of connection to France. Will and Ken had visited together, Ben married a French woman, and Monty's mother was French. They might not have known Louis Lutz, but there was still a link there.

The limo dropped us off in front of the Marché Couvert. With its tall, arched windows and stepped facade, the hall was an elegant example of Art Deco style. It was an impressive building but new in the eyes of the residents of Villefranche. They preferred the majestic lines of the police station on the other side of the road, which had been built only four years earlier than the Marché Couvert, but in the classic style of the eighteenth century.

Ken pointed out the police station to shine a little spotlight on Jacqueline. While I retrieved my camera bag, I cast an indifferent glance at the building, but then something piqued my interest. On the stairs leading up to the entrance, I spotted Apolline. That morning, she'd denied seeing her son, who had definitely been in the village, and now she was exiting the police station in Villefranche? Surely there was something going on. But was it any of my business? I'd been set to have a look at Louis Lutz's files on her behalf, but that had not worked out. Was there something else I could do for her?

At that moment, however, Monty led us into the Marché Couvert, and I had to focus on doing my job. Instead of the usual stacks of fruit and vegetables, the stalls were replaced by tables full of books, writers flogging their works, and publishers trying to make a name for themselves. Things were so busy that the three famous faces hardly got noticed at first. In the throng of people, I stuck to Monty as well as I could, trying not to get too many other faces in my pictures. Despite the trouble with Louis Lutz, I still loved doing this assignment. All of the guys had seriously enjoyed doing what they were here for. Monty's eyes lit up as he took me around the various stalls and pointed out things that I might like.

'The French love their thrillers – they call them *polars*. And it looks like there are plenty on offer, so even Ben might not be wasting his time here.' He stopped to pose for a selfie with a fan. We only made it two stalls further when he had to pose for another selfie, this time with an author who wanted him to hold up his book. When I checked the picture for sharpness, I spotted a familiar person in the background. I lowered my camera and stared at the tear-streaked face of Apolline. She hadn't seen me yet, and I was contemplating whether I should go to her.

'*Coucou, Juju!*'

Relief made me send up some silent thanks. My mother couldn't have chosen a better moment to find me.

'*Maman!* Just the person.'

My mother stepped around me, hugging me in the process. Then she spotted my camera. 'Oh, are you working?'

'I am, actually. But I could use your help. Or rather, Apolline can.'

Maman frowned. 'What do you mean?'

'I saw her coming out of the police station just now, and she doesn't look too happy.' I discreetly pointed at the woman browsing a stall on the other side of the path.

Compassion was followed by determination on my mother's face, as she crossed over to Apolline and hugged her tightly. Though I was supposed to be taking pictures of movie stars, I dawdled and listened in on their conversation.

'What's wrong, *chérie*?'

Apolline took several deep breaths before she could answer. 'It's Constantin. He's out to ruin himself. You know these gang wars the papers have been full of? He's right in the middle of them. Well, maybe not in the middle. He thinks he's in the middle, though. He says he's important to these people. But now the police have picked him up, and they're not going to let him go, because he says he's an important figure in the organisation. They must know he's a nobody. But with this man dying in Saint-Maurice...'

'What does that have to do with Constantin?'

'Nothing! At least, I don't think so. I want to believe the best of him, but he's making it so difficult. I know he knew Louis Lutz, but I don't think Lutz was, you know, blackmailing him. As far as I know, he wanted to work with him on something, but that was years ago. He's now been mixed up with these gangs for months. And frankly, that worries me much more. I wish he'd stayed in Paris. He may not have got up to much good, but at least I didn't know about it all.'

She suddenly straightened. 'Look, I'm telling you this in the strictest confidence, you understand? It was a moment of weakness. Don't you dare exploit me, or your days as mayor are over.'

My mother recoiled. 'How could you think that?'

I huffed quietly. My mother didn't know Apolline the way I did. But I'd heard enough. I rejoined Monty and dutifully clicked away while considering what I'd heard. So that was why Apolline had acted so peculiarly. Sad as it was that her son had taken the wrong path, it didn't look like he was guilty of any of the wrongdoing in Saint-Maurice. Of course, I knew he wasn't the person writing on my window as that had been a woman. And I shouldn't be thinking about the death of Louis Lutz as that had nothing to do with me. But for once my curiosity got the better of me.

Ben, Ken, and Monty lined up in my vision, picking up items from two adjoining stalls, and I took the shot. All these film stars with connections to France, if not to this region itself... it all seemed a bit too coincidental. Everyone had been acting oddly: Apolline and her son, though that was now explained; Isabelle of course; Catherine had been on edge, but that might be explained by the book I'd found at Lutz's house; even Beau had disappeared today with no explanation of where he was going. Not that he was accountable to me for everything he did, but he usually told me anyway. I—

There she was again! Anne-Bonny. She'd found us yet again. I could see her a few paths over, talking to Tiana of all people. How did she know where we would be? I hadn't even told Tiana, though I'd been quite sure my writer friend would be here, amongst her book-friends. But though I was now almost sure of Anne-Bonny hacking into my accounts the way Franck had done, I couldn't remember if I'd even made a digital note of our itinerary anywhere. Did she have a spy in the hotel? And if she *was* working with Franck, did *he* have a spy in the hotel?

A cold sweat broke out on my forehead. Franck had been out of jail for four months now. He had not made good on his promise to kill me yet. I was trying not to let his threat get to me, because worrying about it for the rest of my life would effectively end it too. But seeing Anne-Bonny everywhere I went didn't help my peace of mind. If I was going to stop worrying about her and do my job, I had to know. I tapped out a message to Tiana. *Ask her how she knew to be here.*

I saw Tiana point out something on one of the stalls and while Anne-Bonny looked at it, Tiana stole a glance at her phone. She sidled up to Anne-Bonny at the stall, so I couldn't see if she said anything, but Anne-Bonny turned to her and laughed loudly. Tiana's face stretched into a big grin and she slowly shook her head. When Anne-Bonny was distracted by something, she pulled out her phone again. *She's your neighbour. She followed you, you* nouille.

I stared at my phone screen, feeling my cheeks slowly heat. All right, I supposed me being stupid was also an option. I didn't even dare look at Tiana again and focused instead on Monty. He was in conversation with one of the booksellers, who spoke broken English to him while he answered in broken French. The language did not prove a barrier in this case, though. They were both very excited about the subject. The book in question had a cover with mostly text on it, so I couldn't work out what genre it was. The bookseller tried to tell Monty it was an underrated gem. He was probably just trying to sell the book, but Monty agreed and filled in some details. The bookseller raised his eyebrows and gave an appreciative nod, then took the book back.

'I know, you know.'

Tiana had appeared between Monty and me, and I'd never heard her sound so threatening. At first I thought she was talking to me, but she was, in fact, addressing Monty. 'Don't act so innocent. It was you.'

Monty started, his gaze flitting between Tiana and the book he'd just returned to the bookseller. The man regarded Tiana with undisguised interest.

'Oh, don't worry, I won't tell anyone,' Tiana continued. 'But I know.'

She turned and stalked off, leaving Monty staring at her back, his handsome face scrunched up in a frown. He made an attempt to follow her but then thought better of it.

'What was that about?' I asked.

'I'm not sure I should say.'

I frowned, then stared at the crowd that had swallowed my friend. 'Tiana is never like that.'

'You know her?'

'She's my best friend. The romance writer I told you about in the car.'

Monty's face cleared. 'Ah, a writer. That explains it.'

'Explains what? Hang on, I'm getting her back.' I took a step, but Monty put his hand on my arm.

'Don't worry, it's nothing to do with everything that's going on here. It's this book.' He pointed at the book the seller was still holding. The hand on my arm slipped around it now, and Monty dragged me off to a quieter corner of the hall.

He squeezed his eyes shut, rubbing his forehead. 'I wrote that. And it's terrible.'

That was the big secret? I had no words. Tiana had made it seem like there was something terrible in Monty's life, but all he did done was write a bad book? To Tiana that may have been blasphemy, but compared to the bad things I'd seen people do, writing a bad book wasn't even near the list.

'I think you should be proud of yourself. You wrote a book, how many people can say that?'

'Did you miss the part where I said it was terrible?'

I shrugged. 'My first shoot was terrible too. I'm sure your first role in acting didn't go the way you thought it would either.'

To my surprise, Monty laughed out loud. To my bigger surprise, the sound tickled my belly. I didn't know how Tiana could be angry with him. The man was seriously attractive. I'd already forgotten my curiosity about Apolline and my embarrassment about Anne-Bonny. I just wanted Monty to laugh again.

'I'm sure it didn't,' he said. 'To be fair, I was only three years old, and all I had to do was pet a dog in a dog food commercial. I've learned my lesson though. Writing is not for me. I will stick to the one book and keep reading those by others.' He put his hand on the small of my back and led me to another book stall. He talked about the various books on offer and I completely forgot that I was supposed to take pictures of him. When my mother appeared at my side with that special look that said 'I know what you've done, but if you are going to pretend you don't know, I'm not going to tell you, but I am going to judge you and possibly punish you', I realised Monty's hand was on my waist and I'd let it rest there.

If Léon had been there, he would probably have been hurt by how close I was to Monty, but because it was my mother trying to not look disapproving, my rebellious side wanted to show her there was nothing to approve or disapprove of. 'Find anything good?' I asked, now extremely aware of Monty's hand.

'Just the one book.' She held up a leather-bound volume. 'The others were quite tatty.'

One book.

17

I won't tell you again

Like the one book Louis Lutz had had lying around. One book. One painting. One photograph. And one hand-crafted diamond painting.

How had I forgotten about that? Madame Dufaux had taken it home before I came along the second time. She'd pointed out the painting, but I'd forgotten there was also a diamond painting.

'Monty, this is my mother, the mayor of Saint-Maurice. *Maman*, this is Monty Egg. You probably knew he was coming, but here he is. He likes books too. Talk to him. I'll be right back.'

Leaving my mother and Monty to make an awkward acquaintance, I ran off, dialling Madame Dufaux's number.

She picked up almost immediately. 'Did you find a new clue?'

'Maybe. That diamond painting Monsieur Lutz made, can you take it out of its frame? There might be something on the back of that.'

'Oh, I see. Do you want me to do it now?'

'Yes, please.'

I heard her running up some stairs and putting the phone down. There was some more rustling, and then her voice came from slightly further away. 'You're right! There's a birth certificate and an employment contract.'

I held my breath. 'What's the name on those papers?'

There was a pause. 'I can barely read it.' The click of a light being switched on. 'Looks like... Perret? Perrot?'

My stomach clenched. 'Could it be Parrot?'

'Yes... Yes, that's it! Do you know them?'

I closed my eyes and sighed. Yes, I knew them. 'Thank you, Madame Dufaux, you've been a great help.'

I hung up and immediately called Jacqueline. 'Where are you?'

'Near the entrance. What's wrong?'

'*Bouge pas.* I need to ask you something.'

I more or less fought my way from the back of the hall to the entrance where Jacqueline was waiting with Ken at her side. 'You know you asked me for that list of women who were fifteen or younger at the time Will was here?'

Ken's expression turned dark at the mention of Will's name, but Jacqueline ignored him. 'Yes?'

'It would probably help if you knew what Will was up to during his time here. Did he come to Saint-Maurice or did he stay in Villefranche? Because the list of women who live in Saint-Maurice now but could have been in Villefranche then is going to be different from those who stayed in our village their whole lives.'

Jacqueline pulled up one corner of her mouth as she glanced at Ken. 'I actually met both of them when we were doing a raid in an illegal gambling house. Ken was mortified, but Will only thought it added to the adventure. Knowing him, I doubt he would have seen the attraction of a rural French village. What do you think?' She turned to Ken, whose narrowed eyes and thin lips betrayed a guardedness on behalf of his friend.

'Are you still going after Will?'

'Villefranche, I think,' Jacqueline answered her own question. 'That's as rural as Will gets on his own.'

I nodded. 'That's what I thought. I think I know who painted on my window.' I checked my watch. 'It's almost five now, so I'll have to wait another half hour before I can go and talk to her. She'll be at school, picking up her kids. Do you think I should tell Dupin and Rouletabille?'

Jacqueline shook her head. 'Unless it has something to do with Louis Lutz's death, I don't see any reason they'd have to or even want to know about this. Your window is hardly a priority for them. They're looking for a potential murderer. That can't have been her, can it?'

'Highly unlikely. But I do want to ask her about it.'

Monty and my mother came over and joined us. 'Have you solved it?' Monty asked. 'Do you know who sent the chocolates?'

'Not that, but I have a pretty good idea who wrote on the window.'

'Oh, that's marvellous as well. Let me go and get Ben.'

I held up my hand. 'No, you stay here and enjoy yourself. There's nothing any of you can do to help me with this.'

'But those words were meant for us. I'd like to know which one of us.'

'Ah...' I hesitated. Monty interpreted my silence correctly since he looked at Ken, who threw up both hands.

'I give up. You all seem to be determined to blame Will.'

Jacqueline put a hand on his arm. 'You can't get around the evidence, Ken. I heard him talk to this woman myself.'

'So there's a woman who doesn't like him. That doesn't mean he's killed someone.'

'Nobody says he has. Nor intended to. But you have to admit his silence is quite damning. Let Julie talk to the woman and we'll speak to Will afterwards.'

Ken still seem less than happy about it but he agreed to come with Jacqueline to her apartment for a drink. Monty joined them as well since he had lost the taste for books for the day. My mother grabbed my elbow when I went outside and held up my hand for a taxi.

'Don't be silly, I'll drive you. But have I missed something? Has there been another murder?'

'No, *Maman*, nothing like that. You know the man who died on the *pétanque* court?'

'Monsieur Lutz?'

'Someone sent him poisoned chocolates. They're not what killed him, so there was no murder. The whole affair has nothing to do with any of us, or them.' I gestured at the movie stars behind us. 'But they're getting all worked up about it. Monty bought some of those chocolates for Will Rice, which he is upset about. But Ken is Will's friend and he doesn't allow anyone to speak ill of him. Will also knows the woman who's painted my window, but since I have now found out who that is, I'm going to talk to her.'

'You know her?'

'So do you. It's Sophia Labouche, née Parrot.'

Sophia's face clouded over as soon as she saw me at the door. 'Come in.' She gestured to the kitchen where young voices could be heard. 'I've just fed them, so we have about ten minutes. You figured it out then?'

I nodded. 'I think so. But I'd rather you tell me.'

Sophia sighed as she sat on the spotless couch. 'You know what I used to do. The poker games. Only, I started long before you knew about it. I always looked older than I was, so when I got hold of a fake ID, I thought it'd be an easy way to start earning some money. I had pretty good skills in the game. I think the guy who hired me suspected my ID was fake, but as he already ran an illegal poker game, he was hardly in a position to point the finger. Besides, I knew what I was doing. I was making him loads of money, so why would he care?'

I winced. At the time, I'd admired Sophia for having the guts to get a job taking money from grown men who were drinking heavily. That's the way she'd told it, at least. But by then, she'd been of the legal age to do so. Now, it seemed more reckless than anything else for a young girl – even younger than I'd always thought – to willingly get mixed up in illegal gambling.

'By now, you probably know that Will was at one of those games. He wasn't fooled about my age for an instance. He wasn't the one who blackmailed me, but he kept teasing, making suggestive remarks. Lutz must have been there too. I didn't see him, but he wasn't as conspicuous in those days. He got hold of my birth certificate and my contract, such as it was. Fortunately, he didn't go to my parents to demand money. I think I would have been in even more trouble then. He knew Will came from an influential and wealthy family in England, so he talked to Will instead, demanding that he pay for my transgression. At first, Will said he had nothing to do with me, but he had to admit that if he hadn't teased me, none of it would have come out. Still, he refused to talk to his family or hand over any money. Eventually though, the threats stopped. I thought Will must have paid after all. But as soon as it was announced that Will was coming to Saint-Maurice, I found a note in my purse saying, "I still have them. Unless you want your husband to know, pay up." I couldn't let Raphaël find out! He only knew me as what I am now. He always said he fell in love with me because we were so different – he a daredevil and I so grounded and caring. So...'

'You blamed Will.'

'It was his fault! He should have just left me alone. Now, I had to pay for something I did fifteen years ago. And he got away scot-free yet again. I just wanted him to leave.'

'So you left him a message.'

'Yes, and I'm sorry it was your window. But he had to know.'

'You were overheard talking to him.'

She blanched. 'Look, I will pay you for any damages, but please keep my name out of the media. Think of my children!'

I smiled at what seemed like an overly dramatic reaction to me. But then, she'd been living in fear of being found out for some time. The volcano of guilt and fear that had been quietly rumbling inside her had erupted, resulting in the message on my window. 'Sophia, I have no reason to drag your name through the mud. Now that I know what happened, I don't even mind the window. But you were angry with Louis Lutz and he died just afterwards.'

'I didn't do that!' Sophia shook her head vehemently and waved her hands. 'He was dead. On the ground. I found him that way.'

I grabbed her hands to calm her down. 'I believe you. I only wanted you to know how it looks. And to ask if there is anything I can help you with?'

Sophia thought about that. 'Apart from keeping things quiet? I don't think so. Raphaël has no idea. He knows I found Lutz, of course, but he doesn't know about the blackmailing or what I did when I was young. So he also doesn't know that I was the one writing on the window. He must not know! You can see that, can't you? He trusts me. I can't betray that trust!'

'I won't tell. Just to let you know, though: Will refused to implicate you in anything. He made himself look very guilty in the process.'

'Oh.' She fell silent for a few moments. 'That's decent of him. He... I heard he had his own trouble with Lutz, but I'm grateful he kept quiet about me.'

I left Sophia silently in thought on the couch. She only blinked when I got up and said goodbye. In the hallway, I met a slightly perplexed-looking Raphaël.

'Oh, are you leaving? I didn't know you were here. I wanted to thank you for looking after Sophia. She hasn't been the same since that... since she found him. It's been... difficult to watch. I wish there was something I could do, but I don't want to make matters worse.'

I smiled in sympathy, but once I was outside walking back to my house, I thought the whole thing over. Did everyone in this small village have a big secret? The fact that Louis Lutz made a living from them almost convinced me they must.

In the kitchen, I found Beau's list of our suspects. I'd been able to cross off Madame Dufaux, Apolline, and Isabelle. Now, I could add and remove Sophia at the same time. Of our four famous guests, I could exclude Will and Monty. But now that I knew who had written on my window, there was really no reason for me to keep investigating. Louis Lutz had died of natural causes, and it was up to the police to find out who had sent him the poisoned chocolates and ruined his face.

Just when I was ready to relax and enjoy the rest of my assignment, my phone lit up with a message. *I told you to stop looking. I won't tell you again.*

The cheek! To hide your own identity and then tell other people what to do, that would irk me at the best of times, but after the conversation I'd just had, I'd like to meet this anonymous know-it-all and give him a piece of my mind. Still, I didn't reply to his message. I was above that.

What I did do was put my forefinger and thumb to my temple and gather my angry thoughts. I wasn't going to let this person ruin a perfectly good afternoon, so I pulled the string of indignation from my brain and flung it into the hallway. If I picked it up when I went out later, I'd deal with it then.

The front door opened and in stalked Thibault. He dove into the fridge for a beer, opened it – this time with the provided opener instead of the edge of my kitchen table – and sagged down on a kitchen chair, looking decidedly smug.

'I,' he announced, 'have single-handedly apprehended a murderer.'

18

Stay a bit longer

They had been quiet for too long. Jacqueline had offered both Monty and Ken a drink, but neither of them had accepted. She'd hoped to have Monty's help in convincing Ken that his other friend might not be as innocent as he wanted to believe, but they'd hardly spoken a word since they arrived at her apartment. Monty had made the necessary polite remarks on her taste in interior decoration, which she'd graciously accepted but not believed, and they'd had a short conversation on the recent gang wars, owing to the newspaper that had been on Jacqueline's dining table. With that out of the way, they had been staring quietly at the various items around Jacqueline's flat. Though they were all thinking about the same thing, none of them dared broach the subject. They'd even found places to sit that were as far apart from each other as they could get. Ken was on the couch near the window, Monty dawdled near the door, and Jacqueline perched on a chair at her dining table.

'I suppose we should let Ben know where we are,' Monty said as he retreated to the little hallway to make the call.

'Have you heard from him?' Jacqueline asked as soon as Monty was out of earshot.

Ken ignored her question but addressed the bigger issue. 'Look, Jacqueline, I'm not an idiot. I know that whatever Will did for me also helped him. But he's always been there for me, despite that. And he's not so bad once you get to know him.'

'Your friends don't seem to like him much either,' Jacqueline retorted.

Ken breathed out. 'He doesn't let his guard down easily.' He paused. 'I know we haven't talked about what's going to happen. I'm beyond thrilled to have found you again. But if we're going to make this into anything more, you will have to accept that he is a large part of my life and he isn't going anywhere. I would love for you to be part of my life too, but I won't abandon him.'

Jacqueline struggled to keep her facial expression impassive. He wanted her in his life. And she wanted to be part of it more and more. It wasn't like Will would be there 24/7. Perhaps she could make more of an effort to really get to know him. 'For the record, I never thought Will sent the poisoned chocolates. That's bound to have been some local person.'

Ken nodded his acknowledgement but didn't answer as his phone rang and he picked up the call.

'Will, how's it going?' He hummed a few times in answer to what Will was saying. 'Yeah, we're at Jacqueline's. Do you remember where that was? All right, I'll share my location. See you soon. You don't mind, do you?' he asked when he'd hung up.

Jacqueline shook her head, and Monty entered the room.

'I'm going to pick up Ben from the market hall. He has no clue how to get here. And guys, let's not let this thing get in the way of our fun, okay? If we just get on with our holiday, I'm sure we'll have forgotten the rotten stuff in a few years, but if we let it spoil our time here, we'll always remember.'

'Wise words, my friend,' Ken answered. 'Sorry your fun got cut short. I mean, if you want, you can get back there now and stay a bit longer. The plan was to stay till closing time at eight, wasn't it? We'll wait for Will and join you later.'

'Sounds good.' With a wave of his hand, Monty left.

'So, what is your plan?' It was a bit of a cowardly question, but Jacqueline also didn't want to put words in Ken's mouth.

'Long term, or short term?' he parried.

'Both?'

'I think Monty's right. We only have a few more days here, so we should enjoy them. And afterwards... well... I will have to go back. We're filming in another few weeks. And I suppose you still have your career. So, has anything really changed?'

'*I* think so.'

'Yes?' He looked her in the eyes. 'So can we at least keep in touch this time?'

'At least.' She tried to keep the emotion from her face but she was sure at least a twinkle in her eyes came through.

Ken pulled up one hopeful corner of his mouth. 'Yeah? Maybe more?'

Jacqueline got up and took a few steps toward him, but then his expression changed. The smile disappeared and his eyes narrowed. 'There is... one more thing.'

Jacqueline's stomach plummeted. 'Oh?'

'Of course, it's to do with Will.'

Right. 'And that is?'

Ken put his hand in his back pocket and pulled out an SD card. 'I did make a deal with Louis Lutz. I bought this off him minutes before he died.'

Uh-oh. 'What is it?'

'They're pictures of Will and the girl Lutz was blackmailing. On their own, these photos are innocent enough, but as an illustration of the whole story, they could end his career. I thought buying this would put an end to Will's problem, but I've only made my own bigger. I mean, this could be a motive, right?'

'If the man had been murdered, maybe.'

'But they're still looking for a potential murderer. That could be me. In theory.'

'Did you buy any *coussins*?'

'We all bought those. They're delicious.'

Jacqueline wanted to deny the possibility that his actions could have negative consequences, but she couldn't say the words. Until her colleagues found the actual potential killer, Ken had made a good case for himself. She held out her hand.

'Give it to me. I'll deal with it.'

She had no idea yet if and how she could ethically make this go away, but she would at least try. With any luck, Dupin and Rouletabille would find their heads and clear the whole mess up before anyone found out about Ken's doings.

'So, when you went to see Lutz, did anything seem off?'

Ken's reply had to wait until Jacqueline had answered the doorbell and let Will in. He greeted her with an uptilt of his chin, which she was aching to punch. But with her new resolve, she squeezed out a friendly greeting. Will reacted with a suspicious frown.

Ken greeted Will, ignoring the uneasy vibes in the room. 'I'm just telling Jacquie about my meeting with Lutz.' He turned back to her. 'I don't know where he got my email address, but he sent me a message saying that he'd be waiting for me. Said I'd recognise him when I saw him because he stood out. I didn't even remember what he looked like, so I doubted the veracity of those words. But when I saw how enormous he'd become, I did recognise him. I had no intention of giving him anything at first, but when he said he wanted to make a clean breast of it, he offered me the card for fifty dollars with the promise it was the original and there were no copies. I have no idea why he would want such a small amount since he'd asked for much more when I was an unknown.'

'No, he asked for Daddy's money then,' Will interrupted.

'That may be so, but he must know we now have plenty of money of our own, so why did he not ask for more?'

'Maybe he knew someone was after him?' Jacqueline asked. 'Did he seem fearful in any way?'

Ken slowly shook his head. 'No, he looked sickly and was very out of breath. Could only form short sentences. He seemed to be in a hurry to get rid of me, but I wouldn't say he was scared.'

'So he said he wanted to make a clean breast of it?' Will now asked. 'That sounds to me like he was making amends of some sort. But in that case, why ask for money at all? If he knew he was going to die, what did he need the money for? Did he do it just to be in someone else's way?'

'I think he was the kind of guy who would do something just to annoy another person,' Ken answered with uncharacteristic negativity. It jarred Jacqueline.

'Even if he thought his life was about to end?' She'd seen plenty of people do unfathomable things, but a stubborn part of her still clung to a hope for innate goodness. That was the part that reached for Ken's sunny outlook like a lifeline. If even Ken couldn't see goodness, that hopeful part felt abandoned.

'Maybe it wasn't that. Maybe someone had something on him and he thought he might have to run, or something,' Will offered.

Jacqueline huffed. 'I think that's a lot of maybes. Do we have anything concrete? Before I was taken off the case, I was talking to a woman who was convinced she'd killed Lutz by poking him with a stale baguette. If you met him just after that happened, it might account for his being out of breath.'

Ken thought about that. 'He was sweating as if he'd been running, but instead of being red in the face, he was very pale.'

'You should never have gone out to meet him, mate,' Will suddenly burst out. 'You should have told me he was after you so I could have done something about it myself. It wasn't your problem to solve.'

Will's words surprised Jacqueline, but her phone pinged and distracted her from answering immediately. *My lead confessed,* read the text from Julie.

'It wasn't your problem either. Julie just talked to the woman whose problem it really was.'

Will froze. 'How did she know? I didn't tell anyone.'

'No, I will give you that.' Whether or not it had been smart to do so, he'd kept the woman's name to himself.

Will gave her a look of poison she'd seen so often in the interrogation room that it didn't bother her any more. Then he rolled his eyes. 'She's always blamed me, but it really wasn't my fault. I should be used to that by now, but for some reason, this guy's the only one who's ever believed me.' He gestured towards Ken. 'Anyway, brought you some sweets.'

He tossed Jacqueline a package that she had to scramble to catch. When she opened the paper bag, there was a box of *coussins de Lyon* chocolates inside.

'You do seem to have a knack for doing the wrong thing.' Did he not realise those chocolates would leave a nasty aftertaste right now?

Ken stirred, probably ready to jump in if Will's faux pas led to a quarrel, but Will shrugged. 'I still had them lying around, and I don't want them now.'

'Maybe you should have thought about whether I would want them.'

'Don't you? Those were the ones Monty bought for me. I thought you'd like to know I still had them.'

'Whether you still had them or not is immaterial. I never thought you would poison chocolates and send them to a local man. I do wonder though... You told that woman Lutz had not been in contact with you. But he got a note to both her and Ken. Is it possible you just missed it?'

Will shrugged. 'Who knows? I wouldn't have been bothered much if he had sent me something.'

'No. Instead, you let Ken deal with it.'

Ken sat up straight at that remark, and Will took a step towards Jacqueline.

'That was my decision,' Ken said at the same time as Will answered, 'I didn't tell him to do that.'

'And you didn't think what the repercussions could be for the woman?'

'I didn't even know anything was going on until she painted "go home" on the hotel window.'

'Did you contact her after that?'

'No, she just sent me a note to meet her in the street after dark. And like a good boy, I went.'

'Yes, I heard. Did you know about this?' Jacqueline held up the SD card.

'What's that?'

'No, I haven't told him,' Ken interrupted.

'What *is* that?' Will finally showed some real emotion. 'I told you to stay out of it. I knew it was a bad idea to get you involved in the first place. I never should have asked you to meet with him all those years ago. You're too righteous. You couldn't have just told him to shove off in the first place. Oh no, you had to make it right. Will you stop making things right for me?'

'If you weren't set on destroying yourself, maybe I could let off sometimes. You're over forty, for crying out loud. You've made it big. You've earned a lot of money. You've got *fans*. I know the charity work isn't just for show. When will you accept that living your own life is more important than getting back at your dad?'

Will's hulky form collapsed. Ken had hit a mark. Wondering what kind of influence his father had had on Will's life, Jacqueline remained quiet. She'd never seen Will care about anything before, but he'd cared about Ken's well-being just now. That alone redeemed him quite a bit in Jacqueline's eyes. She still might not like him much, but she understood Ken's position a bit better.

Will sent Jacqueline an almost docile look. 'So she's in the clear now?'

Jacqueline nodded once. 'Julie's not one to hold a grudge on something as easily cleared up as a bit of paint. So unless this woman sent the chocolates...'

He stared at the rug. 'Those police guys didn't ask me any questions I couldn't answer without implicating her anyway, so I think they're done with me. And with her.'

'Maybe we should just go back to the hotel,' said Ken. 'Would you mind...?'

In answer to that, Jacqueline grabbed her keys. She threw the SD card in her purse, and they all set out towards the car. Will was already getting settled in the back seat when Ken came to stand next to Jacqueline. She rested her purse on the roof of her little hatchback to have her hands free as he enfolded her in his arms.

'Thank you,' he said with that beautiful smile of his. He kissed her, and she forgot all about her dislike of his friend. All she could think of was how to keep kissing him as long as she could. Unfortunately, the kiss ended way too soon, and she poured her limbs into the car to bring the men back to their hotel. It wasn't until they were halfway to Saint-Maurice that she remembered her purse on the roof of the car. She pulled up along the side of the road, but the bag was gone.

19

A picture of a murderer

My mouth took a while to close itself. Beau joined me at the kitchen table, leisurely putting the beer bottle to his mouth.

'You found the person who poisoned the chocolates?'

Beau shook his head but kept the smug look on his face. 'No, I found a different murderer altogether.'

My mouth opened again, but no sound came out. On the one hand, that made more sense, since it was probably the chocolates sender who had sent me a warning just now. On the other hand... 'A different murderer?'

'Remember that painting? The "picture of a murderer"?' Beau made exaggerated air quotes.

I leaned forward and spread my fingers on the table. 'Was it the plant?' I managed, thinking I could steal his thunder with the realisation I'd had at the Festival Botanique. I'd no idea who the victim would be, but I was convinced the intended killer was not the woman in the painting but the poisonous plant in the foreground.

All Beau did, however, was frown. 'What plant?'

I hated when he stole my thunder.

'No, it was Michel Seive.'

I stared at him, feeling like I'd stepped through the looking glass. 'Who? Michel Seive was what? Did Michel Seive send the chocolates? I don't know who you're talking about!'

Beau closed his eyes and shook his head, holding up his hands. 'All right, let's back up a little. You've heard of those gang wars going on in Villefranche, right?'

I nodded, wondering what they had to do with anything. I couldn't stand that he seemed to be in the know while I was in the dark. This was not how we did things.

'With Franck back, things have been a little... shaky, lately. Before Franck went to prison, my father used to run things and Franck would stick to his own agenda. There were always people scheming to get my father's power, but he could easily stay on top. About two years ago, in strolls Michel Seive. Nobody had heard of him, but he was both able and meek enough to be accepted into the organisation. Had all these fancy stories about the crimes he'd committed in Paris and that he was tired of the big city. He quickly made friends with most of the people under my father's command. Never made trouble, did as he was told.'

Where was this going? When I divorced Beau's uncle Franck, I thought I'd done with criminals in my life. I hadn't known Franck was one until it was too late, but I wasn't keen to know more about all the underworldy things going on in Villefranche.

'Then, a year later, his wife was murdered. You probably read about that at the time. The police held a large-scale investigation but they couldn't find any good leads. Michel accused several members of my father's organisation, and so my father held an investigation of his own. Though he couldn't find any clues either and never made any official accusations, that was the start of a division in his ranks.'

I got up to pour myself a glass of juice, then rejoined him at the table. 'Was that when you started to rebel?'

He laughed. 'I was never much of a minion. For that, he had... other members of the family. No, it was more that my father couldn't find the murderer when Michel was sure it must be someone in his organisation. People started to doubt my father's leadership. Instead, they started to follow Michel's orders. Michel was smart enough not to go after the same things my dad wanted, so the two parties coexisted without much trouble for about a year. And then Franck was released. Everyone expected him to join up with my dad. Go back to his job at my dad's cleaning products factory, for instance, to make it seem like he had a legitimate job, like before. Instead, though, he joined Michel's gang. My father was furious, and that started the feud.'

Despite my reservations, I was getting intrigued. 'So what about the murder of this guy's wife? Was that the one you solved?'

'I did.' He smiled, leaning back and crossing his arms over his chest.

'So? Tell me all about it. I know you're desperate to.'

'If you insist.' We grinned in understanding and he moved forwards, resting his elbows on the table. 'So, this painting in Lutz's house. He said it was a picture of a murderer, but I recognised the woman. That woman was not a murderer, since I knew she was in fact the victim of a murder. She was Michel Seive's wife. I was quite sad when she died because she was a really nice woman. She was cultured – liked art and opera. She encouraged me to do more with my drawing. I always wondered why she had got together with someone like Michel Seive, but he kept her in nice clothes and good food.'

Lucky her. All I'd ever been given by my ex was loneliness and regret. Had she known up front what she was marrying into?

'And then suddenly, she was gone. Bludgeoned to death with a blunt object. Michel was devastated. He raged to everyone around him that she had been an innocent, and if they had a problem with him, then they should have come to him instead. But nobody in the organisation had a problem with him. Even fewer people had a problem with her.

'The police eventually decided it must have been a burglar, since some of her fine art pieces were missing. My father devoted quite a lot of time and manpower to retrieving those items, but they were never recovered. And so, her murder went unsolved.'

'Until you saw that painting.'

'I recognised her, and I wondered if the painting had been part of the stolen set. When we were at the Festival Botanique, I saw someone associated with Michel Seive's gang, so I asked him if he could get me a list of the items that were stolen. He was suspicious at first, but I've always remained kind of neutral in the whole situation, so he obliged. Gave me the usual half-hearted speech on defecting but he didn't actually expect me to. I don't know why they still think I could be an asset to any of them.'

I reached out and patted his hand. 'You're precious to me.'

He pulled a face, but then continued, 'As it turned out, the painting was not on the list. Michel had sold it after his wife's death. Whether Louis Lutz was the buyer, I couldn't find out, but it struck me as odd that Michel did not want to keep such a lovely reminder of his wife. But then I thought, maybe Louis Lutz was right. If she *was* in fact a murderer, or had some other murky past, she might have been killed because of that. Michel Seive might actually know the murderer but want to protect him for some reason. On the other hand, why get rid of the painting? And why not go after that person himself? I was ready to give up, but as a last resort, I thought maybe a visit to Michel's house would give me the necessary clues.'

I gave a start that made me spill my juice. 'You talked to him?' Even if Beau had managed to stay neutral, this Michel Seive would have found it pertinent to perhaps hold on to him for a bit, as the son of his biggest enemy.

Beau huffed as I took a cloth from the cupboard and started to clean the spill. 'No, I paid a visit to *his house*.'

'Oh, I see.' I would never get used to Beau's idea of personal space. My key collection gave me a certain feeling of safety. Knowing I could unlock all kinds of prisons, physical or mental, with my keys brought me peace of mind, but he didn't need them to unlock the door to his freedom. A reminder of where he'd come from was always in his back pocket: his set of lock picks.

'Imagine my surprise when one of the items from the list was displayed in full view in his living room. After a bit of searching, I found almost all the other pieces as well. The one item I had not found was the statue depicted in the painting in Lutz's house. But I eventually located it in a wardrobe in the guest room. The only object actually hidden. And then I understood Lutz's remark.'

'The killer was the statue,' I offered, pointing the damp cloth at him.

Beau nodded.

'And Michel had used it to kill his wife.' I wouldn't say it, but I was impressed with his actions and his reasoning.

He only nodded again.

I rinsed the cloth and wrung it like it was Franck's neck. All this talk of murdering criminals was bringing out my vindictive side. I turned back to him, leaning against the sink. 'But how are you going to prove that? You weren't supposed to be in his house to begin with. If you told anyone, they would just say that you had planted the statue there.'

'Fortunately, they didn't do that. It's hard for the police to accuse someone of planting evidence when they don't know who that person is. I sent them a picture of the statue in the wardrobe and told them to look for the missing items in Michel Seive's house. I included the fact that he had sold a precious painting of his wife with that statue and where they could find it. Seive is maintaining innocence, but I've already heard that several of the people supporting him have now gone back to my father. Turns out most of them only sympathised with him because they'd been fond of his wife.'

'So he effectively killed his popularity. And you solved the mystery.'

He puffed up with a glowing smile.

'Well, actually, Louis Lutz did.' I felt very mean as I watched him deflate. 'But you worked it out.' That brought back a bit of his delight, but it only fully returned when I asked, 'And what about the gang wars?'

'With their leader in custody and most of the figureheads defecting, there's not much left to war over.'

'And that's all down to you.'

He was now so full of hot air again, I thought he might float at any second. Still, I felt a strange kind of motherly pride in him. In effect, he *had* stopped the gang wars. That was quite a feat.

'And... Franck?' I didn't really want to ask because I was trying to keep my worries about him from Beau, but since he'd mentioned my vengeful ex, it would seem strange if I didn't ask.

Beau looked me in the eye when he said, 'I don't know.' Then he looked away again. 'He's been very quiet since he announced he would not be joining my dad. I wouldn't say that's suspicious, though. He probably wants to lie low until my dad has come to terms with his separation. He may be family, but my dad can be quite stern when people don't behave according to his rules.'

I knew that was an understatement. Beau had experienced his father's 'sternness' himself. It was one of the reasons he now lived with me. Not wanting to rain on Beau's parade even more, I decided to keep the message from the would-be killer secret for now. If I had to worry, I'd do that later, but for now, I wanted to bask in Beau's happiness.

'I say that's cause for a celebration. The hotel will have some champagne. I think Jeanette can squeeze us in even with the crowd the film stars are drawing. I'm sure they will all want to draw inspiration from your heroic actions.'

20

Maybe he's doing drugs

I followed Beau's inflated chest into the restaurant, still quietly sniggering behind his back. Jeanette had given up waitressing, but all her staff knew to take me to the private room when the restaurant was full. Tonight, two of the four actors were already seated at the table, sharing an aperitif.

'Oh! How did it go?' Monty turned his charm on me, but I was happy to note that, though I still enjoyed his good looks, it did nothing funny to my stomach this time.

'All cleared up,' I declared.

'So, it was about Will, was it?' Ben raised one eyebrow.

I'd been debating whether I would question Ben about the photograph in Louis Lutz's house, but that remark sealed it. 'Will was involved, but there is no issue any more.' I pulled the picture of Madame Tariel from my purse and placed it on the table.

Ben glanced at it, but didn't react. Monty, however, asked, 'Who's the looker?'

'I don't know,' I said truthfully. 'I found it in the dead man's house. On the back, it says Madame Tariel.'

At the mention of the name, Ben did look up. 'It doesn't look very old.'

Before I could ask what he meant by that, the door opened, and Jacqueline, Ken, and Will came in. Jacqueline, though dressed as elegantly as ever when she was off duty, nevertheless sagged on her chair like a sack of potatoes. She delved into her purse and pulled out a piece of broken and scratched blue plastic.

'This is going to get me into trouble.'

I wrinkled my nose. 'What is it?'

'Evidence. That I have accidentally destroyed. But I doubt my boss will see it that way.'

'Evidence for what?'

'Against me,' Ken said while holding up his hand.

'Oh.' That was probably bad.

Beau let out a low whistle. 'Are you sure it was accidental?'

Jacqueline pinned him with one of her stares. 'Yes, of course. I forgot my bag was on the roof, so it fell off when we were on the road. When we found it again, the whole bag was ruined, including the SD card with pictures of Will.'

'No, I mean perhaps you did it subconsciously.'

'Perhaps, but I didn't do it on purpose. And that's the part my boss is going to doubt.'

I gave her a sympathetic look but then shrugged. 'It's not going to do you any good worrying about it now. And hey, you don't have to worry about the gang wars any more. Beau brokered peace.'

They all let out incredulous sounds, and I let Beau have his moment. The moment lasted all through our starters. And while I enjoyed his excitement and the praise the others stacked on him, I couldn't help a nagging feeling that we weren't on dry land just yet. Not with Franck, and not with this attempted murder case. Sure, I'd found the person who painted on my window, but we were no closer to finding out who wanted to murder Louis Lutz, nor how he had actually ended up the way he did. I knew it wasn't my obligation to find out, but somehow, I felt I knew something, or had seen something that could lead me to find the one responsible. And judging by the message on my phone, that person thought so too.

Ben was tapping his fork on the table. 'I wish these people would realise what a decent dinner time is. Who can live on a few bits of charcuterie? I'm ravenous.'

As if summoned, Jeanette brought in the first steaming plates, piled high with Théo's best creations: *tablier de sapeur, andouilette, quenelles,* and *saucisson chaud.*

'I thought you said you didn't know anyone around here,' I said to Ben, who tucked into his *tablier.*

His frown showed the wheels turning, but when he had decided my remark was indeed unrelated to what he'd said, he asked, 'Yes, so?'

'So what did you mean when you said this picture isn't that old?' I held up the photograph of Madame Tariel in illustration.

'Ooh, intrigue. And for once, it isn't me.' Will leaned forwards with twinkling eyes.

'I just happened to know that your Monsieur Tariel is not married, so the only Madame Tariel would be his mother. But the woman in the photo is quite young and the picture doesn't seem old enough for it to be her.'

'Oh, come now, Ben,' Will teased. 'You just happen to know? There's got to be more to it than that. Who is this Monsieur Tariel?'

Ben kept his eyes on his plate. 'Just some local bloke I met at the garden festival. I don't know why you're making a fuss. This schnitzel is excellent. Have you tried it?'

'It's tripe.'

He stopped chewing and slowly put down his fork.

I continued, 'I found this photograph at Louis Lutz's house. When I saw you talking to Monsieur Tariel, I thought you might know who the lady in the picture is,' I explained.

'I'm sorry but I haven't the foggiest.' Ben shrugged.

Will pointed his fork with a piece of sausage at Ben. 'Yeah, I'm not letting you off that easily. We've all shared our secrets. You all know by now I was the reason why Julie got a message on her window. Jacqueline has destroyed evidence of Ken talking to a dead man. Monty wrote his awful book.'

Monty shot up, his eyes wide.

'Oh, please. Like we wouldn't know about that.'

Ben looked from Will to Monty. 'News to me.'

Will turned back to Ben. 'So how come you of all people have found a local friend?'

Jacqueline was the only one still eating. Just before the next mouthful she remarked, 'Maybe he's doing drugs.'

All the others gasped. I was the only one who knew it was supposed to be a joke. 'Jacqueline, that's not funny. She means that my mother has her suspicions about Monsieur Tariel.'

Suddenly, Ben grinned. 'Yes, he told me about that when he saw you this morning. Thinks it's hilarious. Every time he sees her, he tries to be extra shifty.' Then he sighed and put his fork down. 'All right, it was bound to come out at some point. I'm going to quit.'

The others stared at him.

'Quit what?' Ken asked.

'Acting.'

Another round of gasps, even from me.

'I've had a good run. I've earned a lot of money. But I'm not having so much fun any more. And now that I'm going to be a dad...' He trailed off.

'Congratulations,' I said when no one else did. That set off a round of resounding compliments, hand shaking, and laughter. They all agreed it was the end of an era, Hollywood wouldn't be happy without him, lots of women would be sad, and all other kinds of parting words.

'But what does that have to do with this local man?' Monty asked eventually, returning to his pike dumplings in cream sauce.

'He's an estate agent. My wife has always loved this region, so we're thinking of moving here.'

'But you hate the French!' I exclaimed.

Ben's eyes sparkled as he pulled up one corner of his mouth. 'I *am* an actor, you know. I was trying to hide my secret. But I guess it's only right that you all are the first to know.' With that, he picked up his fork and continued to enjoy his food.

'Then let me be the first to welcome you to the area,' I said, handing him the photograph. 'Perhaps you can deliver this to Monsieur Tariel next time you see him.'

He took the picture with a grateful smile, but I had to hide a certain irritation. Again, I'd been taken in by an actor. He'd completely fooled me with his arrogant Englishman act. Could I judge people at all? Well, at least that made for one less suspicious character. As far as I knew, none of these guys had anything to do with Louis Lutz's death. If nothing else, Tiana would be happy.

I glanced around the circle of handsome men. '*Les gars*, I'm sorry to have to ask this, as it's your holiday and everything, and you've been harassed by so many people already…'

They laughed.

'Let me guess,' Monty said. 'You have a friend who loves superheroes. Does she like all of us, or just Will?'

I made big, innocent eyes at him. 'Oh, no, she can't stand you. You met her at the book festival.'

Monty's face fell.

'But I'm sure, if you grovel enough, she will be able to forgive you.' I winked at him.

Will shoved Monty against his shoulder. 'Actually, if Ben is moving to the area, maybe we should do a bigger meet and greet. Get some of the more starry-eyed citizens of Saint-Maurice used to having him around.'

But Ben waved his hands and shook his head. 'No, no, nothing is certain yet. I'm all for throwing Will to the lions.'

Will clutched his heart. 'The things I do for you. I will once again sacrifice myself.'

I watched him for a few minutes as he laughed and joked with his friends. He seemed more relaxed after his talk with the police. Or maybe it was a talk with Jacqueline. Whatever had happened this afternoon, Jacqueline and Will didn't seem so antagonistic any more. Apart from the one misplaced joke, she hadn't said anything all evening. Neither had Ken. All they did was quietly eat and smile at one another. I wondered if that was what I looked like when Léon was here. If so, I should do something about that. It was rather sickening.

The rest of the evening, the guys exchanged brash stories about things that had happened with fans – being sent everything from cross-stitched portraits and not-so-well-travelled birthday cake to voodoo dolls and dirty underwear – and their experience working with different directors. Thibault impressed them with impersonations of various Hollywood people. He also reenacted a scene as Ben's character, The Defier, that made Ben laugh and remark that nobody would miss him if Beau stepped into the role. It was a joke, and Beau took it as such, but I could see the slight change in his expression that nobody else picked up on. I had suggested he take up acting as a profession before, but he'd always waved it off. Now, however, he might see an opportunity for real stardom. On the one hand, I wished him all the best, if this was really what he wanted; on the other, I would miss him something fierce if he went away to pursue it.

At the end of the night, I walked home on his arm. When we passed the big window, I couldn't help but remember the words written on it just two days ago. I still felt sorry for

Sophia, having to live through those anxious moments. I really hoped we could regain our friendship from before. Then I smiled. To think that I'd actually suspected Catherine at one point, when she was using that red paint at the garden festival.

'Have you seen Catherine lately?' I asked Beau.

'Not since the garden festival. Why?'

I shrugged. 'No reason. She was acting strange, but maybe she was just nervous for the festival. Would you go?'

'To Catherine?'

'No, to Hollywood. If they asked you?'

Beau laughed softly. 'They haven't ask me, have they?'

I supposed that would have to do for now. Soon, the actors would be gone again. But they weren't gone yet.

21

I've done something wrong

'They what?' Tiana's eyes bulged over the mug that was now only half-filled with coffee. She hadn't even noticed the spill on her jeans.

'They'd like to meet you.' Being able to do this for my best friend made me so happy.

'Even Will?'

'Even Monty.'

Her nose wrinkled.

'He's really quite nice,' I said.

Tiana's eyes narrowed but then started to twinkle. 'You like him! How can you like... him? He's *beurk*!' She wrinkled her nose again.

'Excuse me? That is a very attractive man.'

'I didn't think you went for that kind of thing.'

I frowned. 'What's that supposed to mean? I'm only human. Or don't you like the way Léon looks?'

Tiana chose her words carefully, which was a wise decision just then. 'I think Léon's extremely nice. But he's not what you would call an Adonis, is he?'

I recalled Léon's face from our call the night before. He'd been so sweet, asking me all about my adventures with the actors, even though I knew he wasn't actually interested in them. Not an Adonis? That all depended on what you were looking for. I thought the receding hairline made him look distinguished. He may not be interested in fashion or surface beauty but he breathed intelligence, and there was dependable loyalty in his eyes. Most of all though, he showed me he loved me every single day.

'It's what on the inside that counts.'

'Says the person taking pictures of the outside all day.'

'Exactly. That's how I know. It's not always the objectively pretty ones that are really the most beautiful.' In my mind flashed a picture of Will Rice, but I didn't want to ruin Tiana's dream.

'And you like the outside of Monty Egg.' She had finally realised that half her coffee had landed on her jeans and was now brushing her lap with her hand.

'Well. I mean...' Was it hot in here? I decided to leave that where it was and changed the subject slightly. 'You need to get over the whole book thing. Why is that such an issue for you, anyway?'

She glared at me. 'Because it's *him*. Do you know how hard it is to get people to read your books? But not for him, oh no. Even though his book sucks egg – pun intended – his publisher has given it every bit of push they could think of. Still didn't take off, of course. Should have used his own name.'

She gave an eyeroll, but I smirked. 'But he didn't, did he? You know he knows the book is bad?'

She blinked at me suspiciously. 'He does?'

I nodded, trying not to relish her change of heart too much. 'Said he'd learned his lesson, and writing was not for him.'

Slowly, Tiana's spitting attitude turned into a dignified calm. 'So, when can I meet them?' she finally asked.

I opened my mouth to answer her, but through the window, I saw Tiana's neighbour Catherine pass by.

'Sorry, I just have a question for her,' I said to Tiana as I got up and opened the front door. 'Catherine!'

She looked my way, gave a small yelp, and hurried along the road.

'Catherine, please, *attends*!' I ran after her. 'Have I done something wrong?'

'*De quoi?* No!' Tears welled up in her eyes and she hid her face in her hands. 'No, it's me. *I've* done something wrong.'

Whatever it was she'd done, I didn't want her to feel she had to tell me out in the street, even if it was a dead end with no traffic. Tiana was still waiting in her open door and she gestured for us to get inside. I put my arm around Catherine's shoulders and guided her to towards Tiana.

'Come in, *mon bijou*. Have some coffee.'

We installed a now sobbing Catherine on the couch and waited for her to explain. It took her a few minutes of quietly sobbing and sipping her coffee before she could talk. 'I've been so afraid.' She sniffed. 'He was just such a nasty man, and I couldn't help myself. But then afterwards...'

Tiana and I exchanged a glance.

'Catherine, did you poison the chocolates?' I asked.

'Poison? Where would I get poison? No, I pushed him. He was sitting on that bench and there was nobody else around. I still think he deserved it. My poor Banzaï was so scared of him. I saw him kick my sweet little pup! I wanted to hurt him there and then, but Daniel stopped me. He knew... he was...'

Wincing, she stopped talking.

'I know about the book. And that Lutz was holding it over you.'

She stared at me, wide eyed, her sobs momentarily forgotten. 'How did you know that? You're so clever.'

Tiana frowned a question at me, but I could only return a reassuring glance.

Catherine cast her eyes down and took a breath. 'Well, if you already know about that, maybe you can understand that we didn't want any more trouble. But anyone who can hurt a defenceless animal is not worth the air in their lungs.'

I could only agree, but I wanted her to give us more. 'So you saw him sitting on the bench above the *pétanque* court. What exactly did you do?'

Catherine pressed her eyes closed. 'I came at him running. I knew I'd need a good bit of momentum to shift him, especially if he tried to fight. Of all the people staring at the hotel... If one of them had looked over their shoulder... I didn't think. I started to run, and then I pushed him in the back. He didn't fight at all. Just launched off that bench and plummeted down the hillside. I... I killed him. Me! I killed another human being. That's so much worse than kicking a dog!'

She wailed loudly, so that she didn't even hear me protest at first. She shrugged my hands off her shoulders when I tried to calm her that way, so I had to shout to get her attention.

'Catherine! You didn't kill him. He was already dead.'

Panting, she finally looked up at me. 'He was... He was? Really?'

I nodded. 'Confirmed by the police pathologist. His eating habits were what killed him. You merely threw his body down the hill.'

Catherine winced. 'The intent was still there.'

'I'm not saying what you did is right, but you did not kill him.'

She took a few deep breaths, alternated by a few last sobs, but my information had calmed her down considerably. 'So... that's why he didn't put up a fight. Maybe, if he hadn't been dead, he wouldn't have moved at all.'

I didn't have an answer to that.

But Tiana chipped in, 'That's entirely possible.'

Catherine straightened and took one last deep breath. 'All right, I will confess. I'm going to go freshen up and then I'm off to the police.'

As soon as she uttered that last word, though, her courage deserted her. Her shoulders sagged and she wrapped her arms around her.

'Would you like me to go with you?' Tiana offered.

Catherine nodded weakly, and I took that as my cue to leave. Traipsing along the path down the hill, I considered what I'd learned. For one, I was glad I was not Louis Lutz. To have so many people hate you that one would throw you down a hill, another would punch your face in, and a third would send you poisoned chocolates... And those were just the people who had actually taken action. I couldn't fathom having even one person hate me that much. Well, apart from Franck maybe. But though he had threatened me, he hadn't come near me since he'd been released from jail. I was beginning to wonder if his time in prison had had an impact on him.

But Louis Lutz had driven three people to violence against him. Now that I'd found out how he'd ended up on the *pétanque* court in the first place, that nagging feeling that I should be able to figure who had ruined his face and who had sent the chocolates returned. Obviously, I could discount Catherine. If she'd sent the chocolates, she wouldn't have taken the chance to be seen in broad daylight pushing a man down a hill. And after she'd done so, I'd seen her run away myself. She wouldn't have had the time to go down to the *pétanque* court before he was discovered.

But now that I knew Louis Lutz had not been hit in the face before he fell down the hill, I realised the weapon must have been wielded by someone down there. Beau's theory that it was a *pétanque* ball seemed more likely by the minute. But then, where had it gone? The police had asked all the players to show their boules and none had been missing. But what else could the attacker have used and where could he or she have hidden it?

Since I was already on my feet and I didn't have a photography assignment to get to today, I decided to walk on to the *pétanque* court and have a look for myself. Then, I stopped, the dust around my feet moving ahead without me in the shade of the trees. I was about to *look* again. After I'd been told twice not to *look*. But I was looking for the face basher now, not the chocolates sender. And since I was almost certain it was the chocolates sender who was checking my activities, would they care if I *looked* into the face basher?

It really had nothing to do with me. I was only *looking* out of curiosity. My window mystery had been solved, and though there had been a link between that and the dead man, nobody would benefit from me examining the scene of the crime. Well, Justice would benefit! Imagining myself with a flying cape, I channelled my inner superhero and descended, in the name of Justice. Had I not spent the last few days in the presence of real-life superheroes? Surely some of their splendour must have rubbed off. I crossed the square and descended the path towards the *pétanque* court rather full of myself and impervious to warning messages.

Now, if was here to play my relaxing game, and I saw the person I hated most in the world either come sailing down or already lying there, would I go and ask for help? It was a question that required soul searching, though I didn't have to think long about who this person might be. But if I found Franck dead somewhere, would I really literally kick him when he was down? I tried to be honest with myself, and I was rather proud of the outcome. I could honestly say that I would not. I'd come a long way in four years, because there was a time when I definitely would have. Therapy was a wonderful thing.

But Louis Lutz had been in the middle of his blackmailing game. And not everyone had the mental fortitude of Isabelle's husband to confess to the people concerned. I didn't think every file in Louis's cabinet was used for blackmail, though plenty were. Those chocolates could have been sent from anywhere, but I believed the person who mutilated Louis face must have been someone local. Perhaps that's what my subconscious was trying to tell me. I could work out who'd done it because I was a local and I knew the other locals.

Still, that left plenty of suspects. Who had I seen on the village square that morning? I racked my brain – my neighbours' faces were so familiar to me that I didn't even notice them. But now, looking around the *pétanque* court, I found a new problem. Whatever the attacker had used to hit Louis's face with, it must have been a convenient object. But the object itself must have been stained with Louis's blood. Where would the attacker have stashed it? The court itself was necessarily flat and open, and there were no bushes around it. On one side, it was flanked by the steep hill running up to the village square. The main road into the village ran along another side of the court, where the entrance was, and on the valley side, a little wire fence protected players from falling down another steep slope.

The only possible place where someone could hide anything was at the end opposite the entrance. The court had been dug into the hill at that point, so the natural curve of the landscape was held up by a concrete wall. However, that wall was markedly lower on the valley side. Even in my heels, I could easily scale it. I entered a little triangle of public land that had once belonged to a vineyard owner, but had reverted to the community when he died. The vines were long gone, but nobody had bothered to clear up the *cadole*, the little stone hut with a wooden door once used for storage. Like so many wooden doors to sheds and barns all over France, this one had decayed on the top and the bottom, leaving large gaps both around and in between the planks.

I half expected the *cadole* to be full of rubbish that people couldn't be bothered to take to the recycling centre, but it was surprisingly empty. So empty, in fact, that there was no way the weapon was here.

'Meh,' I said out loud to no one in particular. I'd thought myself so clever to look in this place, but obviously the police would have checked it too. It wasn't like it was hidden from view. Still, I went inside. The hut couldn't be more than a metre and a half in diameter, but I knew every stone of it. Sophia and I had used it to stash all our treasures. They consisted mostly of sweets at the time, but they were precious to us. I ran my hand over the rough stones to my right. Then I looked down. One of those stones had been loose. That's where we'd hidden all our stuff. I wondered...

I wriggled the stone free and heaved a sad sigh.

22

By then it was too late

For the third time in four days, I found myself on that pristine couch, wondering how she kept it so clean with all those kids running around, while I and my sometimes-cat managed to get hair, crumbs, and whatever else on my couch with no effort at all.

'I'm sorry to disturb you when you're cooking,' I said when Sophia came in with coffee and biscuits, even though I'd told her I'd already had coffee at Tiana's. 'But I thought it best to talk to you personally.'

'You're always welcome here, Julie,' she said warmly.

'Even when I don't exactly have good news?'

She smiled, her eyes on her coffee cup. 'I think I always knew you'd figure it out at some point. I was just so angry, you see? It was such a long time ago, and now it was all coming back.'

'So you'd written on the window. Then what?'

'Yes... I was already in a state of rage. I'd only just bought the paint in Villefranche, so I could paint our shed door. But Lutz and Rice had been on my mind all the while, and by the time I arrived back in Saint-Maurice, I couldn't see straight. I didn't think about the consequences when I was writing, and when I came down to the *pétanque* court and saw him lying there, I actually laughed. Here was the man causing me all this worry. I'd risked my reputation by writing on your window, and here he was, already gone. He hadn't even been considerate with the moment he chose to die. In hindsight, I know how deranged that sounds, but at that moment, it all made perfect sense. I took out one of my boules and threw it at his face. Only then, when I saw the damage I'd done, I panicked. All of a sudden, my reason returned, and I realised I shouldn't have painted your window either. But by then it was too late. People were already gathering around it and wondering what it meant.

'But of course, by then, I had a bigger problem. I took my dirty ball and hid it, and the paint, in the first place I could think of. Then I came back and rolled him over to hide the evidence that his wounds had been afflicted after he fell. At the time, I didn't even wonder how he died, or whether he had died at that spot. All that concerned me was to hide my own guilt.'

She took a few deep breaths, and I used that time to process what she'd told me. She must have felt so isolated in her fear. If nothing else, I knew what that was like and I felt deeply for her.

'Once I'd turned him over and rearranged the gravel to erase the traces of me pushing him, I went back up to the village square to gape at your window with everyone else. But I didn't want to run the risk of someone else finding him, or perhaps finding evidence of me having been there before, so I went back almost immediately and pretended I'd found him then. Those tears you saw me crying were certainly not an act. By then I'd realised what I'd done and that I couldn't undo it. If he had died by someone else's hand, I had probably tampered with any evidence, so I decided the best thing I could do was to keep quiet about everything I'd done.'

She'd kept her eyes on the hands in her lap that closed around each other ever more tightly. Now, she relaxed her hands and looked up at me. 'Even when you found out it was me who wrote on your window, I thought I could still hide my other actions. I told Raphaël that I'd left the paint on the *pétanque* court but that I'd pick it up later. He never questioned me, so I picked up the paint from the *cadole*, but I couldn't see any reason to pick up my boule as well, since I wouldn't need it for a while if I said I had to get over the trauma of seeing Lutz at the *pétanque* court before I could play again.'

She brushed a crease from her skirt. 'So what's going to happen now? I didn't kill him. But my biggest fear is that Raphaël finds out. Or even my children. What am I going to tell them? How can I raise them to do the right thing when I didn't do the right thing myself? Not when I was young and not even now, when I'm older and should be wiser.'

I didn't answer. I didn't know what was going to happen. I was the only one who knew that she was guilty of corpse desecration. If I didn't tell the police, I would be perverting the course of justice, but if I did, Sophia might go to jail. Did I want to be the one to do that to her children?

'So when did you give him the chocolates?' I asked eventually.

Sophia's gaze fell on the green box on one of her shelves. 'You mean those? They're mine. I get them sometimes, as a treat, but I never bought them for him. Why would I? I hated him.'

I nodded slowly. Neat as it might have been, I didn't expect Sophia to first plan a murder, and then be taken by sudden rage and attack him when he was already dead. Which meant that I had to look for yet another person. If I ignored the warning messages.

'Sophia... Did you send me any messages?' Now that I knew just how much she was involved, she seemed the most plausible person to tell me to stop looking.

But she shook her head, not understanding. 'What kind of messages?'

If she'd have sent them, she would have known. '*Tant pis*. Never mind.'

I decided to hold off on telling the police about Sophia's position until either they or I had found out more about the sender of the chocolates. At the very least, that would buy me some time to wrestle with my conscience.

Walking home from Sophia's house, I passed the hotel. Though it wasn't as packed as the day the movie stars arrived, there were still more people around than usual. In all the confusion with Catherine that morning, I hadn't even been able to let Tiana know what the actors had planned. In spite of all Ben's objections that nothing was certain yet, they didn't want their stay here to be remembered solely in connection with the death of a local, so they were working on an impromptu gathering where people could get a little bit closer and they could answer questions and eliminate any lingering negativity about their visit.

Naturally, this was right up Will's alley. Monty and Ken were also up for a short performance and a meet and greet. Ben, however, was less confident that he could put down a good performance without a script. He'd never been very good at improvisation. That's why they wanted to talk to Tiana. If they could rough out an idea for a skit, Ben would be happier to indulge the others and join in. Tiana could help them come up with some sort of script to follow.

Knowing that Tiana was probably still be in the Villefranche police station with Catherine, I entered the hotel lobby to see if the actors were ready for her yet. I had to shout to Jeanette over the buzz of people milling about, but Jeanette informed me that as far as she knew, the actors had not been down yet, not even for breakfast. She'd had someone take up room service to Ben's room instead, where they'd apparently all convened.

At that moment, the buzz intensified as Ben strolled in through the revolving front door. He cast me a knowing grin that confused me. I frowned back at him, but all he did was gesture with his head to follow him upstairs. I gave Jeanette a Gallic shrug but followed him nonetheless.

'You're not going to believe this,' Ben announced to the room when we both entered. The others looked up, Will and Monty from the edge of the bed, Ken from the desk chair, and Jacqueline from her perch on the windowsill next to him. 'What was it again your mother called Monsieur Tariel?' Ben asked me.

'As Christian as the Mafia.'

'Right! I can tell you now, the man is a saint. I went to see him this morning about that house I'd had my eye on, and I gave him the picture you had given me. The poor man burst into tears!'

Commiserating sounds erupted from the room. Both for Laurent Tariel, and for Ben having to deal with a crying estate agent.

I had some trouble picturing the flashy businessman as a blubbering mess. 'Did he tell you why?'

'It turns out the woman in the picture is the love of his life. But his best friend was also in love with her so he moved continents to give them happiness.'

My heart constricted for Monsieur Tariel, and my hand went to my throat as I said, 'Oh, that poor man. But then why did Louis Lutz have her picture?'

'Laurent had never told his friend that he wanted to marry the girl too, and Lutz threatened to let them know.'

'But he's been here for years! It shouldn't matter now if she did know?'

'It does for Laurent. He doesn't want anything to interfere with their happiness. But he was overjoyed to now have her picture back. With the death of Louis Lutz, he knew, of course, that he didn't have to worry any more, but he got rid of all her pictures when he moved here in hopes of getting over her more easily. He never did, and now, seeing her picture was too much for him. He is very grateful to you.' Ben inclined his head to me.

His words warmed my heart, and I decided I must go and see Monsieur Tariel in person soon.

'That's your good deed for the day done,' said Ken. 'But what about the house? Did you get it?'

Ben held up his thumb in answer, and the others cheered him.

'Now all you need to do is break the news to Frederickson,' Monty said.

I'd understood from earlier conversations that he was their producer.

Ben waved away his words. 'Is there any brekkie left? I think I'm just going to stay at this hotel until I've had everything on the menu. It's all delicious.'

They all agreed, but that meant there was no breakfast left, and Ben ordered some more.

'Anyone want to join us for a good long hike after breakfast to walk it all off?' Ken asked.

Jacqueline did not seem too happy with his invitation, but she put on a bravely open smile. Monty said he would, but changed his mind after a shove from Will, which made Jacqueline's eyes smile too.

I finally crossed the room to sit next to Jacqueline in the open window. 'You don't seem so anti-Will these days,' I whispered.

'I found out it wasn't me he was against,' she whispered back.

I frowned. 'What do you mean?'

She shook her head. 'Oh, nothing. Daddy issues. Hasn't seen his father in years, but he's taking it out on the people close to him. I think I can work with that.'

I tried to suppress it, but a small smile escaped nonetheless. Yes, Jacqueline knew herself well. In another life, she must have been a therapist. She was firm but fair. She had no patience for self-pity but she would guide anyone through the deepest cesspool if they let her. If Will opened up to her, they would both end up the better for it.

I glanced around at the happy faces in the room. Jacqueline hadn't laughed so much in years, and Ken kept stealing glances at her and smiling. Ben had just secured a house in the area, Monty seemed like he never had a care in the world anyway, and even Will had loosened up. Still, something didn't add up. If Will had had no contact with Louis Lutz in fifteen years, then why had he been here at Christmas? Or had Raphaël simply been mistaken?

I studied Will for a few minutes as he joked around, until he caught me staring at him.

'Is your friend coming, or what?' he asked.

Hoping he hadn't picked up on the suspicion in my stare, I fished out my phone and called Tiana. She had just finished with Catherine and was only too happy to join us. Monty was the first to go out and greet her, all apologies to her and the wider community of writers. The only redeeming fact he could offer was that he'd refused to let his name be attached to the book. When he'd reached this point in his account, he asked Tiana how she'd found out. She turned bright red and actually sighed with relief when Will rescued her. Though it could have been adoration that made her sigh.

For the next hour they all planned that afternoon's event, but my thoughts were elsewhere.

23

Sunshine. That is what I am.

Word about the meet and greet spread like wildfire, and the village was overrun by people from far and wide outside Saint-Maurice. Social media was abuzz, and since it was a Saturday afternoon, most people didn't have anything better to do than to show up at the Saint-Maurice *salle des fêtes* and shake the hand of a famous actor. Though the building could hold quite a lot of people, I wasn't sure there'd be enough space inside once the four took to the stage to perform the skit they'd thought up with Tiana.

Already there were plenty of people inside, hoping to catch a glance of a famous face before the event began, though most were still wandering about outside, keeping to the shadow side of the building or lounging under trees to avoid the hot sun. Some had brought picnics, and one entrepreneurial ice-cream man had parked his van close by and was doing great business.

Despite the heat of France in July, there was a curious amount of black leather in the crowd. Beau's biker buddies had also picked up on the news that there were famous people to be gawked at. I tried to get a better look at them, sometimes zooming in with my camera. Beau spent a fair bit of time with these people, but he never talked about them, so I was the tiniest bit curious. Most of them were quite a bit older than him. I supposed they had more time to devote to riding around the countryside. Only two of them were closer to Beau in age. One of them was Sophia's husband Raphaël. The other was the husband of my make-up artist, Maile. Gío ran a motorcycle shop in Villefranche, but he'd probably closed up or asked Maile to take over for the afternoon, because the handsome Italian was riling Beau by agreeing with Céline that Frou-Frou was the perfect name for her puppy.

I grinned to myself and went inside, changing the settings on my camera as I did so. The Hollywood posse had come over from their residence in Lyon to make sure things didn't get out of hand. The man named Guy had been on the phone the entire time since he'd arrived. One of the women was trying to get the actors to change but they were having none of it. Will was keeping the crowd busy, and the others just wanted to be themselves for once. I was far from the only photographer in the crowd today, but the others were being directed by yet another member of the posse.

Other than sneaking in studies of Beau's elusive biker friends, I'd made sure to snap some pictures of Tiana discussing the course of events with the actors – she could thank me later – but now that three of them had disappeared back-stage, I kept to the sidelines. Every now and then I held up my camera to see if I could get a good shot of the crowd, but there were too many people to make up a good composition. Event photography was never my forte, unless I had someone to focus on. In this case, my subject should have been Will, if I'd wanted even more pictures of him. In every photo, he was at the forefront of the activity, in his element playing the part of the star.

With the emphasis on playing. In my mind, he was still the most enigmatic of the bunch. From what I'd seen, he seemed to be a grumpy kind of guy, but after he'd talked with Jacqueline, some of the terseness had left him. One moment, he could be withdrawn and almost melancholy, the next he was an all-out extrovert. Which was the real Will?

A small man with dark hair popped out of the crowd. I trained my camera on him to be sure it was indeed Brigadier-Chef Dupin. What was *he* doing here? Other than star-gazing like the rest of them. I lowered my camera and glanced at Jacqueline. A cloud passed over her face as soon as she saw him. In contrast, his face lit up when he saw her. I went over to my friend to form a front in case she needed it.

'You can tell me, was it on purpose?' Dupin asked conspir-atorially, as soon as he came near.

'You know it wasn't,' Jacqueline said flatly.

'Do I, though?'

'What do you want, Dupin?'

'Those of us who haven't been suspended are still looking for a would-be killer.' He glanced around with an air of superiority.

'Look for him elsewhere.'

'Ah! But we believe it will probably be a woman.'

A tiny little twitch at Jacqueline's eye told me she probably suppressed an eye-roll. 'Still on the poison-is-a-woman's-weapon line?'

'You'll see,' he said with a self-satisfied grin.

I narrowed my eyes at Jacqueline. 'What did he mean by that suspended part?'

She stared into the distance, seemingly intrigued by the masses. 'I went to see my boss this morning to show him the ruined SD card. He implied I'd destroyed the evidence on purpose and suspended me pending investigation.'

'Are you serious? He has no evidence for that.'

'I suspect some peer pressure was involved.'

My head snapped towards the little man who was trying not to disappear into the crowd. 'Dupin?'

'Like I said, he's not a bad policeman. At least he wasn't, until the higher-ups made me capitaine instead of him. He seems to be determined to prove them right. But he still has some clout with the commissaire.'

'So when will you be reinstated?'

'It depends.' She hesitated and looked at Ken. 'But actually, I'm not in a hurry.'

I felt like a cat who'd spotted a mouse and I was sure I could catch it. 'Really?' I drew the word out as long as I could, and she chuckled.

'Why make the same mistake twice?'

'But who will I pester when I find another dead body?'

'So stop finding dead bodies. It's not that hard. I know plenty of people who've never found one dead body.'

I could only laugh, and even though I knew she hated hugs, I gave her a big one. 'You've been my sunshine for so long, you deserve a little of your own.'

She huffed. 'Ah, yes, sunshine. That is what I am.'

Our gazes fell on Will at the same time, seeing as he was yet again commanding the attention. This time by standing on a chair, closely ogled by Isabelle, of all people, and announcing the meet and greet would officially start in ten minutes.

I bit my lip to gather my courage, then asked, 'Are you sure it wasn't Will?'

Jacqueline's piercing eyes sought mine. 'It wasn't Will doing what? The chocolates?' She turned her head to study the exuberant figure in the centre of attention. Then slowly shook her head. 'I don't see it. Why do you think that?'

'Just rumours, I suppose. Someone said they saw him here at Christmas, and there were whispers of him having his own trouble with Lutz.'

Jacqueline frowned. 'Ken says he always spends Christmas with his family.'

'But you said he hates his dad.'

'Yes, and the feeling is mutual. Apparently, his dad hides out in the study when Will is there. But he showed me a picture of him with his mother and sisters.'

'All right, then it really must have been someone else Raphaël saw. He wasn't su—'

I stopped mid sentence and Jacqueline tensed. 'What? What is it?'

Eyes wide, I stared at Jacqueline. 'I think I know who did it. But there's no way I can prove it. Unless...'

It was now twenty minutes after Will's announcement, and I had a thorough understanding of what the words nerve-wracking meant. My gaze roamed the crowd now gathered inside the hall, taking in both well-known and unknown faces. The last time I was here had been for my own party, the day Franck was released from prison. Tiana had done a wonderful job then, but the hall had seemed too big for just a simple party. Now, the event organisers had opted to make it standing room only, in order to accommodate more people. This mob was stretching the limits of health and safety guidelines, but so far, everyone seemed to be having fun, casting glances at the stage erected on one side of the hall. Catherine was there, as well as Sophia and her family, and I even spotted Apolline. Isabelle was still around but was now flanked by her husband, who held a firm grip on her hand. Anne-Bonny, of course, was live-streaming the event.

Madame Dufaux sidled up to me. 'Exciting, isn't it? We'll have a real celebrity living amongst us. You don't think he sent the chocolates, do you?' she added with a slight frown.

'Who? Ben? No.'

My assurance seemed enough to take away her worries, as her face cleared and she began chatting away cheerily to her husband, Monsieur Vray.

At last, Ken took the stage, his blond hair dancing in a non-existent breeze. I made a mental note to talk to the make-up lady to see if she could give me some pointers for Maile.

'Bonjour,' Ken said into the microphone and waited for the crowd to calm again. *'Merci,'* he continued with his million-dollar smile, and had to wait another few seconds. 'Thank you all for coming at such short notice. I know it's a headache

for the PR people.' He gestured to the PR posse, who smiled and waved indulgently. 'But I hope you will all enjoy this little event.' He paused for applause. 'Now, we have this down as a meet and greet, so it's probably useful to know who you're meeting. I think you all know this guy.'

He pointed at Will, who entered stage left and stood next to him. The crowd cheered as Ken put his hand on Will's shoulder. 'His name is Will,' he continued. 'And he is...' He looked at his friend.

'Unimportant – go away, Will.'

He shoved his friend's shoulder, and Will held his arms wide, then dramatically slumped his shoulders and exited stage right, where Monty entered.

'It's Montgomery Egg, everyone!' Ken announced, while Will turned on his heel and stalked back to centre stage.

They started a whole spiel about how Will thought he was also important, the other ones claiming he wasn't. And this was my cue to tap Sophia on her shoulder and ask her to take her children outside. I gestured to Raphaël to stay and enjoy the show, but I needed Sophia and her children to come outside, where they would meet Ben, who had donned a deerstalker to show everyone he would be playing his role as the detective. He surprised me by establishing an instant rapport with the children, while I took Sophia aside.

She gave me a slightly uncertain smile. 'Is something wrong? I told you everything I know.'

'It is a meet and greet, after all,' I said, indicating the children. 'They're just the first ones to meet.'

She slowly tipped her head back in acknowledgement, and though she didn't seem entirely convinced, she didn't comment. She joined her children as Monty came out and Ben went inside. I checked one last time to see if the children were all right, but Tiana had come out with ice cream, so I followed Ben back into the building. He had made his own cheered entrance and was now policing Ken, who, according to plan, had accused Will of murder. It was a slightly edgy choice of subject under the circumstances, but it would have been strange not to address the elephant in the room.

Will went all out, widening his eyes and clutching his chest.

'I saw the police talking to you. Why else would they be talking to you?' Ken asked.

'Why would I kill anyone? I'm English,' Will retorted.

This got a chuckle from the French crowd as Ben stepped forward, shaking his head.

'He is not the murderer,' he declared, pointing at Will. 'I wouldn't expect someone like you to work it out.' He pulled up one eyebrow and plucked at Ken's blonde hair. 'But *I* know who the killer is.'

'I don't even know who was murdered,' cried Will.

'Shows what you know. No, no, the killer is...' Ben paused, turning his back to the audience and looking left and right, earning him another chuckle from the audience. Then he faced front and pointed at Raphaël. 'You!'

The rest of the audience laughed. They didn't see Raphaël turn pale. He tried to laugh along, but when Beau and Gío came towards him, he shoved the people behind him to the side and ran towards me and perceived freedom. I tried to block his exit, but he was considerably larger than me, and his momentum sent me tripping backwards and landing on my bottom.

Beau and Gío chased Raphaël out, and I heard gasps and murmurs from the audience inside. Ben, Will, and Ken, however, resumed their skit as though this was all part of the play. In a way, of course, it was, and we'd warned them this could happen, but I had to commend them on their presence of mind. As they continued their act, the audience settled and refocused their attention on the stage.

Rubbing the bruise I was sure was already forming, I scrabbled to my feet and hurried out. Sophia grabbed my arm as soon as I exited, her eyes wide with concern.

'Was that Raphaël? Why are they chasing him? What's going on?'

I put my hand over hers. 'I'm sorry, Sophia. I'm sure he did it to help you, but he did it.'

'What? He did what? But...'

Tiana came over and put her arms around Sophia's shoulders. I'd asked her to step in if she saw Raphaël on the run, as the truth might be better coming from a friendly but impartial person. Also, I wanted to be there when they caught him, so I sent Sophia a look of sympathy, then turned away. In the parking lot, someone shouted and a motorcycle engine growled to life. I skidded round the corner, the gravel throwing up a cloud of dust around my shoes.

A third biker was running after Raphaël as he sped away on a motorcycle. 'That's my bike!'

Thibault planted his fists on his hips, staring at the disappearing bike. 'Well, there he goes.'

I couldn't believe my ears. 'So?' I put my hands on his back and pushed him towards the baby blue Harley-Davidson. Was he giving up that easily? Did he not also have a motorcycle? Could he not just as easily follow the escaping villain?

Only when I'd hoisted myself behind him on the motorbike and he'd started the engine, did I remember that I was not this kind of girl. The hoisting itself should have tipped me off that I did not know how to behave around motorcycles. Panicking, I stood up again. But that was when Beau took off and I just managed to grab his shirt to prevent myself from falling off. I plastered myself to Beau's back and held on for dear life as he sped out of the parking lot and followed Raphaël up the road into the hills.

'This is possibly the dumbest idea you have ever had,' he shouted at me.

Then why are you going along with it, I thought, but I was too busy clenching everything to open my mouth. When I dared open one eye, the Beaujolais landscape was flashing past, lush green vineyards making way for the rockier part of the Pierres Dorées. Where was Raphaël going? He had a wife and children, he must know he couldn't get far. Then again, with a life in prison, he wouldn't be able to see them much anyway. Perhaps it made sense for him to try and get away. But did he have to take the most winding road to get there?

With all the twists and turns in the hilly road, we'd barely gained on him. But with every bend, I got more and more aware of the fact that we weren't wearing helmets, or any other protective gear. Beau had taken off his leather jacket as soon as he'd arrived at the *salle des fêtes* and hadn't had time to retrieve it. Shouldn't we just stop and let the police deal with this? I hadn't even taken the time to properly tuck in my skirt; I felt rather like I was posing in one of my own peekaboo photos. At the very least, my legs were getting cold.

The sound of another engine came up behind us, and I recognised Gío's helmet.

'Maybe we should stop,' I shouted at Beau, but he shook his head.

'Gío can take over.' Surely that was the intelligent decision? But Beau shook his head again. Cold legs were no longer a problem. My body temperature rose with indignation until I felt I would spontaneously combust. One tiny bit of power, and he ran with it. Deliberately putting me in danger! He knew I had to do as he said as long as I was on this machine. I had half a mind to pinch him, but I didn't want to startle him and cause him to swerve off the road. This was it. The end. I was going to die a speed devil, chasing a villain to the bitter end.

At last we came to a longer stretch of straight road, and Beau gave the machine free reign. We shot forward and finally gained on Raphaël. Beau even managed to come level with him and I heard him shout to the other man. I couldn't hear what he said, but I could see Raphaël's face on the motorcycle racing next to us, contorted with fear. He frowned and shouted back at Beau. The motorcycle swerved and I clamped my eyes shut, clinging to Beau as Raphaël slowly pushed us off the road. The only thing I heard after that was my own heart beating so fast I was sure it would burst.

'Julie.'

The voice was too soft. If I was still on the back of the bike going at breakneck speed, Beau would have had to shout my name. Had we crashed? Was I in hospital? I couldn't hear the roar of the engines any longer. No wind was rushing past my face. Beau's hands were on my still clenched fists.

'Julie, you can let go.'

I realised I was panting. But Beau's soft voice reassured me enough to open my eyes. I was still on the back of the bike with my arms around my assistant. But we'd stopped. Raphaël and Gío were standing next to us, looking at me with concern. How could Raphaël be concerned for me when he was the one facing prison? That thought reset my emotions enough to loosen my grip on Beau's shirt.

As soon as I let go, Beau swung his leg over the tank and got off the bike, lunging at Raphaël. He grabbed his shoulders and shook the man violently, flames shooting from his blue eyes. In my already anxious state, I touched my lips with trembling fingers. I'd never seen Beau this angry.

'Why?' was all he said. 'You have a wife. Children!'

Raphaël had let Beau's rage come over him without resisting, but now he frowned and shouted back, 'He was hurting her! He wouldn't tell me what he had on her, but I said I didn't care. I just wanted him to stop. He only laughed and said there were more people in her life than me. I couldn't bear to see her pain any longer. I had to do something. But I only made it worse.'

Beau dropped his hands, glancing at Gío, who frowned. 'There was... someone else?'

Both Raphaël's eyebrows rose. 'No. At least, I never thought so. As far as I know, he meant her parents. I sent him the chocolates after I'd laced them with isocyanate paint. But he wouldn't have eaten them. He told me so himself after I had a change of heart and warned him. He said he never ate anything that he hadn't bought himself. But he kept the chocolates nonetheless so he had something on me too.'

24

Will you be all right without me?

'He was a piece of work, that Lutz bloke.' Monty shook his head.

Tiana stared at her plate. 'He must have been so unhappy. Believing that someone would kill him for the things that he'd done, but still not changing his ways.'

'But in the end, he more or less did it himself,' Ken mused. '*Il s'a donné la mort.* He gave himself the gift of death before anyone else could.'

'Suicide by *grattons*,' Will contributed, taking a bite of confit de canard.

We were all gathered around the table in the restaurant's private room for the last evening the actors would be here. The meet and greet had been a success, and we were updating each other on what happened after Raphaël left. The audience had accepted Raphaël's flight as part of the sketch, and the whole afternoon had wrapped up smoothly. Even the PR people hadn't picked up on the fact that their clients had helped catch a would-be murderer, and we were going to keep it that way.

On my turn, I gave a quick account of our chase and subsequent capture of the runaway, though I was quick to add he was more of a victim than a villain. I *might* have left out some less heroic acts on my part, but they had still left their mark on me.

I rubbed my bum. I suspected the pain there was more to do with Raphaël pushing me over, but I still wanted to blame someone. Or something. 'Stupid saddle. You'd think with a name like Duo-Glide, the second person on that bike would have a smooth ride too.'

Beau gave me a bewildered look. 'That name is to do with the susp...' He thought better of explaining and rolled his eyes instead.

'Can't believe we finally had some action around here, and I missed it,' Will grumbled.

'But... why did he do it?' Monty asked.

I sighed. 'He was protecting his wife. He didn't know exactly what was wrong, but he'd figured out Lutz was bothering Sophia, and everyone knew the line of work he was in.'

'Yes, but... how did you know?'

'Oh...' I had to think about that. 'It was something to do with Isabelle. She'd been shouting from the start that she had killed Lutz with her baguette sword, but everyone knew it couldn't possibly have been her. In fact, she was afraid her husband had taken action and she wanted to protect him.

That made me realise the perpetrator might not be a victim themselves, but someone protecting another. At first, I thought of Will, since he was obviously protecting someone, but when Jacqueline told me you had not in fact been here around Christmas' – I inclined my head to Will – 'I suddenly realised that it had been Raphaël who had told me that, and it had been Sophia who'd implied that you had your own trouble with Louis Lutz. It could easily have been Raphaël who had fed her that lie. And once I'd reached that conclusion, I realised the second message I got telling me to "stop looking" came straight after I'd gone to visit Sophia. She was quite upset, so seeing me there must have really spooked Raphaël.'

'So he wanted to blame Will?' Ken asked.

'He had worked out that Sophia knew Will, and not in a positive way. He said he thought Will could afford the lawyers if it came to an arrest, and that he would not be convicted because he was too famous. Besides, there was no real evidence.'

'Obviously. I hadn't done anything.' Will made an impatient gesture.

'Wasn't that partly why she landed in trouble in the first place?' Ben remarked, concentrating on his *salade Lyonnaise*.

Will didn't react, but I saw Jacqueline cast him an attentive glance.

Beau swallowed a sip of wine. 'Dupin has thrown the book at both of them, but I think they will claim extenuating circumstances. Also, apparently one of the top lawyers from Lyon has taken on their case for a remarkably reasonable fee.'

He left that hanging in the air, and the only one who didn't understand the implication was Lucas, Tiana's boyfriend, who had hardly touched his food and could only stare at the celebrities present.

Though I still thought he was a bit of a creep, I'd gained some more respect for Will. The lawyer had assured me he would at the very least get Sophia off with no jail time, so she could be there for her children. That, for me, was the most important thing Will had done to right his wrongs.

'So, last day. Have you enjoyed your stay here?' I asked to change the subject.

They all chuckled.

'It's been interesting,' Monty said.

'I came away with a new house.' Ben wiped his fingers on a napkin.

'I came away with a girl.' Ken gave Jacqueline yet another heart-eyed smile.

'I also came away with that girl.' Will grinned. 'But as a new friend. And I want you to know, if there's anything I can do to help with that suspension...'

Jacqueline shook her head and waved a dismissive hand. 'Oh, I quit.'

I gasped. She'd told me earlier that she wasn't in a hurry to get back, but I hadn't expected her to throw away her career as easily as that.

She smiled at me, almost apologetically. 'I'm going to take my chances somewhere else.'

Ken put his hand around her waist and kissed her cheek. He couldn't wait to whisk her away, but my insides felt empty.

'You're leaving? When?'

'I'm not *leaving* leaving. Not yet, anyway. I'll be back in a few weeks. Ken says he won't have much time for me when they start filming.'

Small comfort. I needed her. She'd grounded me for so many years. How would I survive without her? The dinner conversation went ahead without me. I drank my wine and ate my food, but I didn't taste either. I tried to be happy for my friend, I really did. She was probably making the right decision. And anyway, it was her decision to make, and I shouldn't even be part of it. But since I was me, I cared about how *I* would feel about her leaving, as well as how good it would be for her.

'What will the police do without you?' Tiana asked.

Jacqueline laughed. 'Maybe Beau can take over. He's done such a good job with the gang wars.'

'Maybe I'm coming with you to America.' Beau wiggled his eyebrows. 'You're not the only one who might need a career change.'

I had just taken a sip of wine that now entered my wind-pipe as I gasped even harder. My thoughts stopped as I fought for air. Coughing, eyes watering, I stared at him. By the time I could speak, tears were rolling down my cheeks. 'You're leaving too?'

He only laughed. 'Don't worry, Juju, I'm not going any-where yet.'

'But when you do, you have my number.' Monty expertly scraped his plate with a piece of baguette.

Wiping my cheeks and still panting, I saw Beau give an answering grin. They had been talking about this, Monty and Beau. That meant there were plans. Again, I'd always known Beau wouldn't be with me forever, but I'd got used to him. They all ordered dessert, but I wasn't hungry any-more.

At the end of the evening, Beau and I walked back home. 'Time for you to go back to your own bed. The wasp fumes will have cleared up by now.'

He hummed acknowledgement, a beatific expression on his face.

'What about Céline?' I said, suddenly peeved. 'You didn't come to Saint-Maurice just for me.'

He stopped walking and raised his eyebrows. 'Julie, I'm not leaving. All I did was keep my options open. You yourself have told me to use my acting skills. Why not take that chance when it presents itself? But now is not the time. The only place I'm going is, as you say, my own bed.'

My anger deflated, and I was left with my earlier melancholy. Would I be scared once Beau went back to his side of the courtyard? Though I hadn't heard from Franck in ages, I had to admit having Beau close had given me a deeper sense of security. Against Franck or against locusts invading my bathroom...

As if he'd read my mind, he asked, 'Will you be all right without me, *ma petite sauterelle*?'

'Don't call me that. The thing was huge!'

He laughed at me! What, did he think I couldn't do without him? Next time I had an emergency, I'd think twice before calling on him. I was a strong woman. So what if he left! You know what? I'd take my chances.

Other books by Christa Bakker

<u>Other books in this series:</u>

Death by Naked Ladies

Beaujolais Blood

The Cold Case: a Vintage Murder

Sieste in Peace

The Gift of Death

Second Hand Murder

Sign up for a FREE Christmas story at

<u>https://christabakker.com/newsletter</u>

Acknowledgements

Another book, another wave of gratitude. Without the people supporting me, I could never have made it to five books in this series!

My thanks to Kristen Tate, my wonderful editor at The Blue Garret, for guiding me in the right direction.

Thank you to my wonderful writing friend Carole Marples, for listening to me whine and sigh throughout the process, and to my mother, for always cheering at my work.

My amazing husband and children deserve my love every day for keeping me so happy.

And thank you to you, so very much, for reading this book!

Editing by Kristen Tate at The Blue Garret

Book cover by Christa & Erik Bakker

1st edition 2025

ISBN: 978-1-916998-11-7

Visit the author's website at: www.christabakker.com

www.ingramcontent.com/pod-product-compliance
Lightning Source LLC
Chambersburg PA
CBHW050601190726
48283CB00007B/2235